Penguin Crime Fiction
Editor: Julian Symons
Money from Holme

Michael Innes is the pseudonym of J.I.M. Stewart,
who was a Student of Christ Church, Oxford, from
1949 until his retirement in 1973. He was born in
1906 and was educated at Edinburgh Academy
and Oriel College, Oxford. He was lecturer in
English at the University of Leeds from 1930 to
1935, and spent the succeeding ten years as Jury
Professor of English in the University of
Adelaide, South Australia.

He has published twelve novels and two volumes
of short stories, as well as many detective stories
and broadcast scripts under the pseudonym of
Michael Innes. His *Eight Modern Writers* appeared
in 1963 as the final volume of *The Oxford History
of English Literature*. Michael Innes is married and
has five children.

Michael Innes

Money from Holme

Penguin Books

Penguin Books Ltd, Harmondsworth,
Middlesex, England
Penguin Books Inc., 7110 Ambassador Road,
Baltimore, Maryland 21207, U.S.A.
Penguin Books Australia Ltd, Ringwood,
Victoria, Australia
Penguin Books Canada Ltd, 41 Steelcase Road West,
Markham, Ontario, Canada
Penguin Books (N.Z.) Ltd, 182-190 Wairau Road,
Auckland 10, New Zealand

First published in Great Britain by Victor Gollancz 1964
First published in the United States by
Dodd, Mead & Company, Inc., New York, 1964
Published in Penguin Books 1966
Reprinted 1969, 1976
Copyright © J.I.M. Stewart, 1964

Made and printed in Great Britain by
Richard Clay (The Chaucer Press) Ltd, Bungay, Suffolk
Set in Monotype Times

Part One

1

The Sebastian Holme Memorial Exhibition was being held in the Da Vinci Gallery, just off Bond Street. The Da Vinci, the proprietor of which was a certain Mr Hildebert Braunkopf, had never been understood in the trade to enjoy more than a modest prosperity. Until, you might say, today – the day of the Holme private view.

There could be no doubt of what was happening today. Certainly Mervyn Cheel hadn't been in the Da Vinci five minutes before he realized that this was the artistic event of the season. He didn't have to look at the pictures to grasp the fact. (For that matter, there was such a crush that the pictures would be hard to fight one's way to.) He had only to look at the people who had given themselves the trouble to turn up.

At many affairs of this kind members of the public were inclined, he supposed, to nudge each other, point at *him*, and murmur 'the distinguished critic and pointillist painter, Mervyn Cheel'. (Just at the moment, he was covering Art in a provincial paper for a financially nugatory consideration: a disadvantageous circumstance which he would explain as arising solely from his exceptional professional integrity.) But at *this* affair, Cheel had soberly to admit, the nudging (if there had been elbow-room for it) would have been mainly prompted by others. Several sorts of big people were here. And they hadn't turned up because the absurd Braunkopf, in an Edwardian frock-coat and a gardenia probably intended to suggest the late Lord Duveen, was dispensing champagne somewhere at the back of his rather poky premises. They had come because they believed – whether on the strength of informed judgement or of fashionable tattle – that Sebastian Holme's paintings were eminently worth buying.

7

But the champagne wasn't to be despised. Cheel began to edge in its direction. A couple of glasses would carry him on nicely till luncheon. And then, with luck, he might find among the sillier part of the crush some art-struck woman who would offer him a meal. His northern newspaper was unsympathetic to his representations about an expense account. Most impertinently, it had offered instead some species of voucher which he could exchange for a snack in a milk-bar. He doubted whether it fobbed off its financial correspondent (or even its parliamentary correspondent) in *that* fashion. Which just showed how, when you were dedicated to Art, you had to play your own hand in a pretty ruthless way. Yes, a free feed would be convenient.

He continued a crabwise progress through the room. Every now and then the crowd would part for a moment and he would catch a glimpse of a picture. Many had little red labels attached to them already, and some bore cards which he knew must announce their acquisition for some national collection. Between this room and the next he paused to inspect, pinned to the wall, a list of the prices which Braunkopf was thinking proper to ask for his current masterpieces. He stared as he read – for the figures seemed unbelievable. You could imagine them attached to Cézannes and Renoirs, or to some absolute top craze of the moment, like Jackson Pollock. Yet the Holmes were undoubtedly selling, and the actual sums must be at least in some relation to those thus announced. How had Braunkopf done it? There was only one explanation. He must have begun by getting a couple of rival American collectors into the market, and thus established a yardstick at the start. Once you managed that, it seemed, there was every chance of the most inflated prices holding up and hanging on.

'Hullo, old boy, hullo!' A corpulent man in City clothes was shouting at Cheel across a sea of women's silly hats and jostling bosoms. 'Not seen you since St Tropez, eh? How's dear old Meg?'

Cheel scowled. He was unencumbered by a dear old Meg; he had never been to St Tropez, which was doubtless the most vulgar of plushy resorts; and the corpulent man was totally unknown to

8

him. Observing, however, that the corpulent man was holding high above his head two perilously brimming glasses, and conjecturing that he was prepared to bestow one of these upon anyone acknowledging his acquaintance, Cheel let his scowl melt into a glance of gay recognition. 'How are you, my dear chap?' he said. 'Yes, I'll be delighted.' He edged forward a further two feet, and the glass was in his hand.

'Cheers,' the corpulent man said, and drank.

'Cheers,' Cheel said with distaste, and drank too. The effect was almost instantly invigorating. 'Big crowd,' he added with civility.

'And the stock selling like hot cakes, eh? But I got one, all the same. Rang Braunkopf before market hours. This fellow Holme, it seems, was knocked out while still among the young entry. By niggers, too, somebody said. Poor show, eh? But as soon as Debby told me the story I got on the blower. When a *great* painter dies at that age – well, you damned well can't go wrong. Eh?'

Cheel was on the point of saying something rather rude (he disliked a coarse and mercantile approach to Art) when he observed that the corpulent man, who had long arms like a baboon, was actually within reach of one of Braunkopf's magnums. He contented himself therefore with holding out his glass.

'Cheers,' the corpulent man said, when he had done what was required of him. 'Mind you, my own interest is naturally in growth yields. So I have them do me a lot of security analysis. "Guestimates", as those chaps like to say. Ha-ha.'

'Ha-ha,' Cheel said. He had taken half the second glass at a gulp.

'Mind you,' the corpulent man said, 'although you fix it on the blower it's always wise to come along and check up. Even if it lands you in a bloody long-haired crowd.' The corpulent man stared broodingly at Cheel for a moment, as if measuring the length of his locks. He appeared to arrive at some favourable – or at least charitable – decision. 'Old boy,' he said, '– care to come out and have a bite on Debby and me? L'Aiglon, perhaps. Or the Caprice. Or Pipistrello, if you've a fancy for it. And, of course, dear old Meg too.'

For a moment Cheel hesitated. The proposal held its substantial temptation. But the hazards were obvious. Debby might not be so vague about her St Tropez acquaintance as her husband was. And Cheel might find himself, when questioned, improvising a totally implausible Meg. 'Thanks a lot, old boy,' he said. 'But I have a luncheon date, worse luck. Love to Debby, though.' He proceeded to edge his way on in the crush. 'At the Mansion House,' he added over his shoulder, and for good luck. The corpulent man, he was gratified to glimpse, seemed sobered and impressed.

There was, of course, some sort of Sebastian Holme legend. Holme had died in circumstances which could be represented as romantic or at least picturesque. Cheel had been slack on his homework of late, and he didn't know much about it. But the corpulent man had been referring to it in his crude talk about being knocked out by niggers. Cheel had known Holme at one time. Indeed he had enjoyed, or suffered, what must be called an encounter with him. But the fellow had gone abroad and been forgotten about. Perhaps he had sent work to be exhibited in London in a small way now and then. Perhaps he had contrived the beginnings of a reputation as an exotic painter, a sort of latter-day Gauguin.

Anyway, it had all been unimportant, and there had been no occasion for a distinguished critic to take any cognizance of it. But now there was *this*. Mervyn Cheel continued to edge around through *this* with a mounting sense of annoyance and even indignation. He had to acknowledge a lurking and vexatious feeling of being a little out of it. Lord Crawford appeared to have forgotten him. He received rather a bleak nod from Sir Herbert Read. Kokoschka patted him in a kindly way on the arm as he went by, but plainly because he had mistaken him for some Central European *émigré*. When he made too sharp a turn and awkwardly jabbed in the stomach the Director of the Metropolitan Museum in New York, the Director, although taking this winding in good part, seemed indisposed to make it a basis of conversation.

Being thus put a shade out of countenance, Cheel decided to retreat from the ephemeral spectacle of mere humanity to the sempiternal world of art – or at least to that world to the extent that it was embodied in the work of Sebastian Holme. He began therefore to fight his way towards the pictures. The process wasn't without beguilement in itself. Since the mere humanity assembled in the Da Vinci Gallery was preponderantly female, and since the jam had now reached something like rush-hour density on the Underground, the obstacles to be squeezed through in the quest of this aesthetic refreshment were constituted largely by *les tétons et les fesses*. A little ingenuity was thus enough to lend a curious interest to his progress. Only once, however, did he positively venture to *pinch*. This was when he felicitously found himself edging between a plump girl and the *Direttore* of the *Pinacoteca di Brera* in Milan. If the girl squeaked (he thought happily as his finger and thumb closed) the *Direttore*, being Italian, would get the blame.

Flushed from this exploit, Cheel found himself standing in front of one of the largest of Holme's canvases. So far as quality went, he knew already, of course, approximately what he was going to see. All these grandees weren't here for nothing, and Holme's fame must already have gone abroad in a manner that he himself had somehow missed out on. All the same, he was unprepared for what hit him now.

He was looking at what might be called, perhaps, a jungle scene. It was full of horrible greens which had been made, somehow, to suggest intolerable heat. There were blue shadows, not receding harmlessly from the picture plane but menacingly reaching out at you. And in two tremendous places Holme had triumphantly modelled deep into mysteriously luminous tunnels through the fiercely proliferating vegetation which was his subject. There wasn't much to be said in front of the thing except that

England had decidedly never had an exotic painter of this stature before.

Mervyn Cheel was almost abashed. If he hadn't taken a firm grip of himself his spirit might simply have been rebuked before the painting's sheer power. And yet it wasn't in the least a bravura piece. The underlying geometry was faultless, and there wasn't a passage that hadn't been calculated in millimetres. That was no doubt why Sir William Coldstream (whom Cheel now perceived to be his left-hand neighbour) was studying the picture with concentrated attention.

The sense of irritation which had been mounting steadily in Cheel was now reinforced by a strong feeling of injustice and deprivation. Largely endowed with intellect and sensibility though he was, his nature was perhaps a shade lacking in that final generosity which can only rejoice in the good fortune of others. Cheel too was an artist – even if an artist on the critical and analytical side. Who was Sebastian Holme (whose recollected features now rose vividly before him) that all this success should have come to *him*? The man had been (he now clearly remembered this too) an ignorant and undisciplined dauber – neither more nor less. And now *this* had happened. Holme was the sensation of the year; Cheel had to cadge meals and drinks.

He was not left long with this wholly sombre view of the matter. This was a *memorial* exhibition. Sebastian Holme was *dead*. Whoever was in the gravy as a result of this affair, it wasn't that young oaf (he would still be quite a *young* oaf) Holme. He had once (Cheel now remembered) taken what you might call a smack at Holme. Indulging himself in a reminiscent grin at this, Cheel, for some reason, made a half turn towards his right. He thus became aware that he had a right-hand neighbour (rather a close neighbour) too. He took a glance at this neighbour, and the grin froze on his face.

There couldn't be a doubt of it. The man next to him was Sebastian Holme.

12

2

As was not unnatural in such an exigency, Mervyn Cheel fell for some seconds into considerable confusion of mind. It is quite usual (he found himself reassuring himself) for artists to attend their own private views. Yes (he found himself replying), but dressed in their best clothes, standing before their best picture, and assuming whatever pitiful simulacrum of the manners of a gentleman they think may soften up the boobs and suckers who are being introduced to them. And *alive*. Not *dead*.

At this point a cold shiver ran down Cheel's spine. He turned to his left, with the blind intention of making some desperate appeal to Sir William Coldstream. But Sir William had disappeared. So – he saw, glancing wildly round – had Lord Crawford, Sir Herbert Read, and the Directors of the Metropolitan and the Brera. Perhaps he had imagined all these distinguished persons. Perhaps he had imagined – He turned cautiously to his right again. Sebastian Holme was still there.

With a staggering gait, and all oblivious of the pleasures of letting a hand or thigh brush those so-enticingly-circumjacent female posteriors, Cheel made his way to one of the Da Vinci's over-stuffed and moth-eaten plush settees, sank down on it, and endeavoured to collect his thoughts. He positively could not believe, he found, that he was in the grip of simple hallucination. The idea was too utterly repugnant to his just intellectual pride. Only stupid and besotted people *see things* in that vulgar sense. He remembered having read a book called *Human Personality and its Survival of Bodily Death*, and in the light of this recollection he took a cautious glance across the room. But the figure before the jungle painting failed at all convincingly to suggest a Veridical Phantasm of the Dead. It suggested nothing at all except plain Sebastian Holme.

13

There remained only one explanation on this side of sanity: the very obvious one of mistaken identity. It was something that was constantly happening, after all. Why, only a few minutes ago the corpulent man had been taking him for somebody with whom he had once painted jolly old St Tropez red. So here was somebody *like* the late Sebastian Holme. The thing was as simple as that.

Unfortunately – and this seemed the really terrifying fact – the figure was *not* all that like Sebastian Holme. It couldn't be, since it was heavily bearded, whereas he had never known Holme other than clean-shaven – or at least in some slovenly approximation to that state. What had happened was that, quite contrary to at least superficial appearance, he had received a convinced *impression* that this was Holme. And surely this wasn't how simple mistakings of identity worked.

But there was something more. For this something more Cheel found that his mind had to grope. His first conviction had been powerfully confirmed, but he had already forgotten how. He was in contact – his high intelligence immediately helped him to realize – with some element within himself of psychological *trauma*. Something else had come under his observation, and it was something the recollection of which was painful to him.

That! Suddenly he had remembered. But, even as he did so, he doubted as well. There was therefore nothing for it: a confirmatory examination must be made. Almost fearfully, he took a further glance around the room. His first observation was disturbing in itself. It was of the young woman at whose deliciously plump *derrière* he had so lately taken that carefree pinch. The young woman was looking angrily about her. It appeared likely that the Director of the Brera had got away unaspersed.

The bearded man had moved on. He was now standing before – and seemed to be rather furtively, or at least uneasily, examining – *a portrait of a bearded man*! Cheel, although he felt his head fairly swimming before this further *bizarrerie,* managed to get to his feet and wriggle once more through the crush. What he believed he had seen he must see again. Indeed, he must *touch* it. The concurrent testimony of two senses was something which it would surely be irrational not to accept.

The bearded man had again moved on. The picture he was now examining appeared to be of some sort of barbaric dance performed by luridly painted savages. It was another remarkable performance – so remarkable that Cheel, despite his extraordinary situation, found himself in some genuinely aesthetic engagement with it as he advanced. It wasn't that this instantaneity of whirling bodies and flailing limbs had been ingeniously frozen into a complex decorative arabesque, as in some amusing hunt or battle, say, by Uccello. It was rather that from this world of gesture, an irrefrangible *stasis* or solemn timelessness had been educed. Hulking Tom in the Tropics, Cheel thought – recalling, with his customary erudition, just what, in Italian, *Masaccio* means.

This release into professional musing lasted only for seconds. Then he was up against it – and up against the bearded man. The bearded man held a catalogue in his left hand. He wasn't consulting it (why should he, since he was the painter?), but was holding it more or less in the position of a fig-leaf. His index finger, middle finger, and thumb were employed on the job, the catalogue being gripped between the first and second of these, and the third being inserted among the pages. Cheel took one glance at the area of the bearded man's hand thus exposed (it lay, of course, at the triangular base of the index finger and thumb), and what he had already remembered returned to him in fresh, and painful, detail.

He remembered the party – although he couldn't, naturally enough, remember who had given it. He remembered the girl whom (under the clever cover of withdrawing to relieve himself) he had ambushed in the alcove at the top of the stairs. He remembered the manner – embarrassing yet at the same time stimulating – in which the little trollop had decided to struggle and scream. He remembered the firm line he had consequently

15

adopted (the excitement of a bogus rape was, of course, what she had been after) – and then he remembered the impertinent intrusion of the young dauber, Sebastian Holme. Fortunately there had been a bottle to hand; fortunately (or unfortunately) the vigour with which he had himself grasped and swung this had resulted in his shivering it against a banister. What had been left in his grasp (like the *tronchon* in the grasp of a medieval knight who has broken his spear) remained a weapon formidable enough. He had brought it down on Holme's left hand. At least he had managed that, before Holme had laid him out.

And there, before him, was the scar. He could almost see it, as he looked, dripping the blood it had once dripped. If he'd only got the *right* hand – he found himself reflecting – and if, at the same time, he'd got the tendon, he might effectively have cooked the goose of Sebastian Holme's genius.

'Excuse me – but I wonder whether I might glance at your catalogue?'

Cheel couldn't have told whether it was in a sepulchral croak or in the casual but well-modulated accents of a cultivated Englishman that he uttered these words. But he made no mistake about the accompanying action. Without waiting for a by-your-leave, he reached out as he spoke and took the catalogue from the bearded man's hand. And he did so with a slight clumsiness that allowed a finger to brush lightly over the vital spot. Its report was unequivocal. There could be no question of mere visual hallucination. The small, hard cicatrice was palpable to the touch.

Since he lacked the resolution to venture a straight glance at Sebastian Holme, Cheel was unable to tell whether the man had taken alarm. He himself continued for the moment simply to be dead scared – although indeed there may already have been dawning in the recesses of his capacious mind the staggering realization that he was on to something in a big way. He managed to contrive some sort of appearance of consulting the catalogue for information on the painting before him, and then to hand it back with a muttered word. After that he moved away – as expeditiously as the crowd of gazers and gapers would permit. It was the characteristic of Holme's right fist, he seemed to remember, that it came rather rapidly from below, and that its impact on your jaw had the effect of lifting you some inches off your feet before dropping you with a brutal absoluteness on your back.

But he mustn't now let Holme out of his sight. This fact, coming to him with all the mysteriousness of a categorical imperative, had the effect upon him of that first quiver of the curtain which speaks of the imminent unfolding of some vast and exciting drama. Very definitely, his mind was beginning to work.

He had retreated – but to a strategic position from which he could command (as he brought his analytical faculties to bear on the situation) the only public exit from the Da Vinci Gallery. He had so retreated when – with a dastardly lack of all advertisement – he was struck a violent blow on the face. The pain was considerable, and filled his eyes with tears. The bewilderment (since Holme must be a dozen paces away) was extreme. And then he heard a voice. It was a woman's voice, and what it said was, 'Poisonous little man!' His eyes cleared; for a moment he saw the plump young woman before him; her gloves were clasped in her right hand; he realized that what he had been subjected to was their application to his person with much the force of a whip.

A number of people had, inevitably, witnessed this untoward incident. They reacted variously. Some made distressed, shocked and deprecating noises. Others looked away and pretended not to have seen. One or two males placed themselves obtrusively before their womenfolk, as if to protect them from outrage or occlude the spectacle of vulgar violence. But nobody intervened, and within seconds catalogues were being consulted again as if nothing had occurred.

But, for Mervyn Cheel, something more disastrous than a mere passing public humiliation *had* occurred. Sebastian Holme had vanished.

3

There was no point in rushing from the building. Whether or not Holme had departed in alarm, he would by now be swallowed up in the traffic of London's West End. At least – Cheel noticed – the woman who had perpetrated the atrocious assault on him seemed to have departed too. The reasonable course would be to retreat into the next room, discreetly screen himself behind his catalogue from any residual curiosity, and think the thing out. Already, indeed, he *was* thinking. He was thinking that the mystery had a future for him.

The second room was largely an affair of drawings, sketches, *gouaches* and watercolours, together with a few early and quite undistinguished experiments with *collages* and *papiers collées*. Holme having died young (only he *hadn't*), his total output would have been small anyway – in addition to which a fire or some similar catastrophe had rather more than decimated what there was. The catalogue said something about that, and Cheel must clearly study it with attention. Meanwhile, there were preliminary bearings still to take.

What came first into his head – oddly, perhaps, but then he did possess a high degree of literary cultivation – was the opinion of Aristotle in his treatise on Tragedy to the effect that Discoveries made by way of Scars (or External Tokens, like Necklaces) are inferior to Discoveries arising from the Incidents Themselves (whatever that might mean). This might be true about trinkets, Cheel thought, but no competent policeman would back the Stagirite in playing down the solid utility of a precisely located and ineradicable bodily sign. That gash on Holme's hand had certainly needed stitches, and somewhere a medical record of it must exist. It might be one means, if required, of dragging Sebastian Holme back to life screaming.

But why had the fellow decided to be dead? How many people

knew he wasn't? Who was he *being*, if he wasn't being Sebastian Holme? It was all highly mysterious. And the more one looked at it (Cheel found himself reflecting hopefully) the more did it appear decidedly shady. This was the thought uppermost in his mind when he became aware that the proprietor of the Da Vinci Gallery was advancing upon him.

'Ah, the goot Mr Cheel!'

Mr Hildebert Braunkopf, upon whose spherical form the straight lines of his newly acquired frock-coat sat with grotesque effect, had extended a pudgy hand to Cheel on his settee. Cheel accepted momentary contact as a matter of distasteful necessity. He didn't at all care for Braunkopf's tone. To be invocated as the good Mr Cheel was, in form, a totally unnecessary tribute to his moral probity; in fact (he was indignantly aware), it was a piece of damned patronage. Until the present notable *coup* he would only have had to stick his head inside the obscure Da Vinci place to have this awful little man crawling. But now the Duveen image was decidedly in control. Braunkopf was directing upon Cheel the affable condescension to which that Napoleon among art dealers might have treated a minor and temporary assistant to his henchman the late Mr Bernard Berenson. The realization of this naturally prompted in Cheel a strong feeling of hostility towards Braunkopf. Hostility in its turn bred suspicion. And suspicion provided at least a working hypothesis. Whatever the shady business he had come upon might be, Braunkopf's was probably the mind behind it.

This sudden and fruitful thought seemed to make a certain temporizing civility expedient. Cheel therefore said something to the effect that Mr Braunkopf's current exhibition appeared to be a gratifying success.

'My goot Cheel, that, for the Da Vinci, is all in the veek's vork. All our puttikler choice exhibitings are assisted at by the importantest figures the great vorlt of art. You have had the champagnes, yes?' Braunkopf, Cheel noted, didn't import any genuine interrogatory quality into this. Rather he made a briskly dismissive statement of it. Cheel, even if worth a little affability, definitely didn't rate the broaching of another bottle. And Braunkopf was glancing round as if in search of some less expensive gratification. 'What shames,' he said, 'it being a little too late to introduce you my goot freunts the Keeper of the Kink's now the Queen's Pictures, the Chairman the National Art Collections Funt, the Trustees the National Gallery, Mr Onassis, Mr Gulbenkian Two, Mr Mellon Four. All my very goot close freunts, no.'

No – Cheel thought – was the correct word. It would have gone for Mr Rockefeller Six as well. Controlling himself, however, he murmured that these would have been pleasures indeed. Braunkopf, he discerned, was in an exuberant and expansive mood. Considering that he must be clearing thousands, this was only natural. Perhaps the circumstance could be exploited to winkle some vital information out of him.

'Dr Braunkopf,' he asked respectfully, 'were you associated with this remarkable Sebastian Holme for long before his death?'

This bold conferring upon the proprietor of the Da Vinci Gallery of academic distinction *honoris causa* was a success. Braunkopf beamed. He even made a gesture – ineffective, indeed – in the direction of an elderly and battered waiter who was tottering round with a bottle.

'Misfortunately, no,' he said. 'This puttikler prestidigious genius Holme went before, alas, before ever contacting high-class puttikler fully ethical concern like mine.'

'Went before?' Cheel repeated.

'Passed out. Was dropped to rest.' Braunkopf made a gesture of vaguely pious and even liturgical character. 'Entered into –'

'I see. By the way, just how did he enter into it?'

'Enter into it?' Braunkopf appeared bewildered in his turn.

'Into eternity, or whatever you were going to say. How did the man die – if he *did* die?' Cheel snapped this out with the sudden vigour of a pouncing barrister. But Braunkopf merely looked surprised.

20

'How did Holme die, yes? But it is all there, my goot Cheel' – he leant forward and tapped Cheel's catalogue – 'or nearly all there. It is a little softened on account the high-bred feelings all these nobles gentry delicate ladies my goot clients.' He gestured largely about the room. 'Holme was assinated, my goot Cheel. He was assinated in a revulsion.'

'He was *what*?' For the moment Braunkopf's peculiar species of ultra-demotic English had Cheel beaten.

'In Wamba. First there was a Fascist revulsion. Then there was a Communist revulsion. And after that there was the revulsion of the Moderate Democrats. That was the worst, yes? The Moderate Democrats assinated Holme in the Wamba Palace.'

'You mean that this assassination took place during some sort of palace revolution?'

Braunkopf looked puzzled. He also looked slightly restive, as if feeling that the unimportant Cheel had already received more than a fair share of courteous attention.

'The Wamba Palace,' he said, 'was the hotel. The European hotel. The Moderate Democrats burnt it. And cooked the cooks.'

'They *what*?'

'In the ovens, yes. The cooks and the scullions. Also some quite few the guests. It was the end of an exciting day, and the Moderate Democrats were peckish, no? Almost this most prestidigious painter of all time was cooked too. But happily his body was reupholstered, yes.'

'They recovered Holme's body?' Brandy rather than champagne, Cheel felt, would be the welcome recruitment at this moment. His inside wasn't standing up well to Braunkopf's cheerful recital of these horrors.

'The body, yes. But that is small consolation, Cheel. For what is a mere mortal rusk? Oaks to oaks, Cheel. A fistful of dust. Better they had saved all those other immortal *chefs-d'œuvre* this puttikler eminent genius now exclusively exhibited by pre-eminent Da Vinci Gallery.'

'You mean those savages cooked some of Holme's paintings

too?' Cooking paintings, Cheel darkly thought, was probably something that was precisely Braunkopf's own line. 'He'd stored a lot of his pictures in this rotten tropical pub?'

'Holme had arranged an exhibition in the lounge.' It was almost in a tone of delicacy that Braunkopf disclosed this low-class and unethical course of conduct on the part of the unhappily deceased painter. 'All was looted, burnt, trampled by heffalumps, fed to sacred crocodiles in one puttikler great monstrous outrage. Result: all the authentic high-value vorks Sebastian Holme extant in the vorlt today visible to one prestidigious *coup d'œil* Da Vinci Gallery.'

'Do you mean you own the things? You've bought them from Holme's executors, or whatever they're called?'

Braunkopf shook his head, suddenly a sobered man.

'There is a viddow, my goot Cheel. Misfortunately, she and her husband were deranged.'

'They were *both* deranged?'

'But natchally.' Braunkopf was puzzled. 'He was deranged from her, so she was deranged from him. But there was no divorcings, not even any legal separatings, no. So this goot Mrs Holme inherits his estate. Da Vinci simply has high-principled ethical arrangement conduct all sales commission forty per cent.'

'I see. But that wouldn't apply to anything that couldn't be proved definitely within Holme's estate at the time of his death?'

'Supposings not.' For the first time, Braunkopf looked a trifle suspiciously at his interrogator. 'But that is nothings or almost nothings. Holme, my goot Cheel, is *here*.' Braunkopf gave another of his large waves around the room.

'I'd call that hotel business quite lucky, eh?' Cheel found himself momentarily prompted to frank utterance. 'Scarcity value is half the racket, I'd say, in an affair like this. If there proved to be twice as many Holmes in the world as people think there are, then the prices of your lot here would drop by precious nearly a half.'

'But my lot, my goot Cheel, is all almost every one sold already.'

Braunkopf, having announced this with simple glee, seemed suddenly to remember his ethical principles. He raised an admonitory hand and addressed Cheel seriously and with a certain *hauteur*. 'But that is commercials, my goot sir. That is mere financials unworthy professional personages concerned only with enriching the voonderble vorlt of art.'

'Oh, quite so. Your principles do you credit.' Cheel spoke coldly. Humbug in others was repugnant to him. 'Is Mrs Holme, by the way, here now?'

'Supposings not.' Braunkopf hadn't glanced round. Instead, he had looked at Cheel with a sudden intensified suspicion.

'She lives in London, I take it?'

'Mr Cheel, these are confidentials.' Braunkopf had stiffened his virtually boneless person as if seriously offended. 'It is like clubs and banks. Puttiklers of clients is not given.' He glanced past Cheel's shoulder, and his face lit up with a cordial recognition suggestive of the sudden espying of a very old friend. 'Lort Snowdon,' he murmured in Cheel's ear – and walked brazenly off in the direction of nobody in particular.

4

It was in some dissatisfaction that Mervyn Cheel relaxed on his settee. The time was nearly one o'clock, and it still looked as if his luncheon must be of his own providing. What was chiefly in his mind, however, was the small success attending his encounter with the absurd Braunkopf. The trouble was that the man appeared to be *just* the absurd Braunkopf – with enough cunning, indeed, to run a hitherto obscure joint like the Da Vinci, but surely lacking in those larger intellectual resources which would be necessary for the contriving of any deep and bold design. Whereas Cheel himself –

Cheel pulled up on the verge of mere indulgent musing. What he had to acknowledge was that he had failed to get out of

23

Braunkopf any information which he couldn't quite easily have picked up elsewhere. And he had been left entirely guessing as to whether or not Braunkopf knew that Holme was still alive. He rather hoped that Braunkopf *didn't* know. The fewer people who did – it was obscurely coming to him – the more there might well prove to be in it for Mervyn Cheel.

But just how? It was only with the eye of faith, so to speak, that he could as yet distinguish on the horizon of the affair the first warm glimmer and glow of likely material benefit. And between him and that comfortable dawn great tracts of darkness still lay. What, for instance – and here surely was the central riddle – had prompted Sebastian Holme to be dead?

Sophocles, it was true (and here, as so frequently, Cheel's generous classical education took a hand), had maintained that no man was to be counted happy until he was precisely that. But Sophocles's ideas were often on the gloomy side, and he had lived in what were, one way and another, decidedly rugged times. Nowadays people did, on the whole, prefer to be alive. And to be dead even in the figurative sense in which Holme was dead must be attended with great inconveniences. It was – again if only figuratively – to have gone underground. And what was the fun of being an underground man?

A man might, of course, do something of the sort for merely freakish reasons – like a prince or husband in an old play, giving himself out to be defunct, or on a journey, in order to potter round in disguise, spying on his principal ministers or his wife. But nothing quite of this sort seemed to fit the present situation. And something else – something a good deal more promising – did!

Discerning this, Cheel was able to feel that real daybreak was in sight. One went *under* ground, in nine cases out of ten, because things had ceased to be healthy *above* it. To be dead was the simplest and most conclusive way of going into hiding that could be conceived. Sebastian Holme had done something so disgraceful that he just *had* to be dead. Probably he had put himself within reach of the criminal law. And it was up to Cheel to discover just how. It was up to him to unearth the facts, and then to make what he could of his knowledge – always keeping a wary eye, of course, on the criminal law himself.

The crowd was thinning. It was easier to see the pictures – and also to see the little red labels on them. Those labels represented a small fortune for sharing out between Braunkopf and Holme's widow. But – unless there was some sort of collusion going forward to which he as yet lacked the clue – the resuscitated Holme himself simply wasn't in the gravy. For the first time in his life (or death), and contrary to all likelihood and calculation, Sebastian Holme's productions were bang in the Top Ten. But Sebastian Holme himself was clean out of the deal. There were all those little red labels. But the man whose talents had, so to speak, sucked them onto their respective paintings could only shuffle in, wearing a false beard (or was it, so to speak, somebody else's beard?), for the purpose of taking a furtive and fearful look at them.

To Cheel, who was disposed to the persuasion that he himself had frequently been cheated of immortal things by a malign fate, there was something poignant and even solemn in this reflection. He felt for, he felt *with* Sebastian Holme – thus so near, and yet so far from, affluence. It also occurred to him that here was the nub of the matter. If you were dead you certainly couldn't make a fortune. It must be doubtful whether you could even command a cheque-book. Holme as he was at present mysteriously circumstanced might well be persuaded of the desirability of a little subsidizing an awkwardly knowledgeable old friend such as Cheel had now become. But Holme was quite conceivably in the same financial situation as Cheel himself: having sordidly to think twice about the cracking of a five pound note.

This was a discouraging thought – or would have been so but for a powerful start of mind by which it was immediately succeeded. If Holme couldn't benefit from his success because he was dead, those who *were* benefiting from it would not be doing so if he were *not* dead. If Holme were (officially as well as in fact) alive, these pictures would still have been *his* property, and so they

25

couldn't have been his wife's to dispose of. Now that most of the pictures had actually been sold the matter was, no doubt, a little complicated. Still, it seemed unlikely that either Mrs Holme or Hildebert Braunkopf would, at this stage, at all welcome any raising of Holme from the dead. There was surely scope for what might be called negotiation in *that*.

Cheel, who might in so many ways have answered to the type of the Prudent Man commended by moral philosophers, paused on this. He was aware of deep waters ahead of him; he well knew that hidden currents might sweep him unawares far off even the most cunningly plotted course. Moreover there was one circumstance – a sufficiently obvious one – which might transmute to the merest cobweb even the most subtle design (to vary the metaphor) that he could think to weave. The *revenant* Sebastian Holme, after all, had vanished. He might have vanished for good.

It would be idle to claim that a dead man was alive, it would be useless to engineer the most brilliant *coup* turning upon this, if you couldn't, in a crisis, lay your hands on him. A moment's reflection, however, suggested to Cheel that he need have no serious misgiving on this score. For Holme, hazardously disguised behind that black beard, had been unable to resist an impulse to attend his own exhibition on the very most dangerous occasion he could have chosen. He must even have gate-crashed it, since admittance today was more or less strictly by ticket, and it occurs to nobody to send a ticket to a dead man. Having thus attended once, Holme would attend again. It wouldn't be in nature not to.

Cheel got to his feet and prowled once more. So far so good, he thought. He had only to be sufficiently assiduous in his own attendance and he was bound to find his man once more. Yet here again there was a difficulty. It would be reasonable to make three or four further visits to the Da Vinci, but after that his haunting the place would begin to look a little queer. Braunkopf – a suspicious type, as little crooks of his sort commonly were – might smell a rat. Frowning over this new problem, Cheel walked to the front of the gallery. There was a big window, partly draped in velvets holding the same moth-eaten suggestion as the settees. But one could peer over these into the street. Cheel did so, with some thought that his quarry might be lurking nearby after all. This seemed not to be the case. But, over the way, he saw something which cleared up his latest difficulty at once. It was a bar of the superior cocktail and champagne-by-the-glass variety, and its dispositions were such that one could drink while comfortably seated and with an excellent view of the Da Vinci itself. In order to secure such a vantage point, he reflected with satisfaction, quite a substantial daily expenditure on quiet drinking would be justifiable.

So far, so good. Cheel turned back to the main room of the gallery, and sat down again. He had not yet read the two or three pages of biographical information about Holme provided in the catalogue. It was very likely that, after the fashion of such things, they were both inaccurate and less than candid. He had better go carefully over them, nevertheless. What was here recorded of the obscure but picturesque final phase of the painter's life would at least serve as a basis for independent investigation. Cheel opened the catalogue. The first page was unrewarding. But his interest quickened as he read on.

5

At the beginning of 1956 Holme spent about a term at the Slade School, and he is recorded there for the Summer Term of the following year. A few months later, however, he was in Africa. Thereafter, until the end of his tragically short life, he was never in England for more than a few weeks at a time.

Sebastian Holme's interest in the Dark Continent had doubtless been nourished for some years by the exploits of his elder brother Gregory Holme, the distinguished explorer. Mr Gregory Holme – whose good offices have in part made possible the present Exhibition – was only two years older than the painter, but already a legendary if elusive figure. There can be no doubt that his powerful personality was primarily responsible for decisions which were to be crucial in his brilliant brother's career. Sebastian was still very young; his character held all the plasticity associated with the artistic tempera-ment at such an age; moreover his entire aesthetic vision as it had yet formed itself was utterly native, so that it might have been reasonable to look forward to his becoming the painter of a new English Romanticism, of

> *cool trees, and night,*
> *And the sweet, tranquil Thames,*
> *And moonshine, and the dew . . .*

(Moonshine, indeed – Cheel thought. But he continued reading.)

The die, however, was cast. Sebastian Holme became his brother's travelling companion – fellow-adventurer, indeed – and his imagination was thus abruptly thrown open to a vast new range of experience:

> *The wind, the tempest roaring high,*
> *The tumult of a tropic sky,*
> *Might well be dangerous food*
> *For him, a Youth to whom was given*
> *So much of earth – so much of heaven*
> *And such impetuous blood.*

But to all this Sebastian's genius was to rise superbly. In a few short years he had established himself as the supreme master of an entirely new territory: a jungle-world swallowing and dissolving in its violent chiaroscuro such human beings as have momentarily hacked them-selves out breathing-space and elbow-room amid its savage prolif-erations . . .

(Blush-making twaddle, Cheel told himself. But some approxi-mation to hard fact seemed to be coming.)

The mighty spectacle of Resurgent Africa was never, to either of the Holme brothers, a spectacle and nothing more. Keenly concerned for the ordered progress of the entire Continent, they took part in numerous enterprises designed to further the economic, and even political, development of more than one territory lately come to independence. In particular, they were the moving spirits in a small but highly significant import business operating mainly on the seaboard of Wamba and among its offshore islands. When, in January 1963, the reactionary régime of 'Field-Marshal' Mbulu and the RIP (the so-called Republican Independent Progressives) was overthrown by what is now the recognized government of Professor Ushirombo and his MADS (Moderate Advanced Democrats and Syndicalists) both the Holmes were present as keenly interested observers in Wamba-Wamba (the capital of Wamba, two hundred miles in the interior). Unfortunately, as is well known, the revolution, while peacefully achieved and enthusiastically received throughout Wamba as a whole, was attended by sporadic violence in Wamba-Wamba itself. Indeed, for some days Professor Ushirombo and his Cabinet were unable to leave the precincts of the Old Colonial Gaol, and the city was in the hands of Terrorists, Students, and Criminal Elements. It was during this unfortunate phase in the political evolution of the Wambian people that the tragedy occurred.

On the night of 18 January the small European community had thought it well to take shelter in the Wamba Palace Hotel – in which, incidentally, Sebastian Holme had arranged a display of a large number of his paintings by way of welcome to Professor Ushirombo, who was to attend a state banquet in the building immediately upon his taking over. To hold such an Exhibition in a mere hostelry or place of public refreshment was surely ill-judged and unbecoming. It was certainly calamitous. There is every reason to believe that 'Field-Marshal' Mbulu (already in exile on the farther bank of the Upper Wam) caused rumours to be circulated in the disturbed city to the effect that Holme's paintings were in fact a collection of propaganda posters commissioned by the universally execrated 'Emperor' Mkaka, leader of the proscribed JUMBO (a terrorist organization the full title of which is totally unknown). The result was a fanatical attack upon the Wamba Palace, culminating

29

in large-scale massacre and arson. As the hotel was a commodious structure fabricated in the main out of platted straw and bituminous mud the conflagration is said to have been spectacular.

Almost the only survivor of this incident – regrettable in point of the loss of life involved, and vastly tragic because of the destruction of more than a score of irreplaceable works of art – was Mr Gregory Holme. Seizing a prog (*a kind of native sword with a serrated blade*) *he cut his way to the bank of the Wam, boarded a* krimp (*a species of native light craft, graceful in construction and probably of Arab origin*) *and constrained the indigenous Wambians forming its crew to set sail down stream at once. After a two-day passage of the dangerous rapids of the Upper Wam (during which, most unfortunately, his crew was without exception eaten by crocodiles) Mr Holme had the good fortune to contact a small but effectively armed mobile column commanded by Colonel Uk, which had been placed at the disposal of UNO by the Lapland army, and which was hastening to Wamba-Wamba to support the legally constituted Government of Professor Ushirombo.*

Returning to the capital thus effectively accompanied, Mr Gregory Holme found that a large measure of order had already been achieved. The charred bodies of those who had perished in the hotel were waiting, gracefully garlanded, to be claimed by anybody who wanted to claim them. The remains of Sebastian Holme, which had escaped the worst effects of the fire, had already been identified. Professor Ushirombo (a close personal friend of both brothers) is said to have broken down when revealing to the survivor one circumstance attending the discovery of Sebastian Holme's body. The painter's current sketch-book was in his pocket, and he had actually recorded in it several brilliant impressions of the fatal attack upon the Wamba Palace. Sebastian Holme was an artist to the end . . .

For the moment, Mervyn Cheel read no further. Instead, he consulted the body of the catalogue and found what he sought: the presence in the Da Vinci Exhibition of a fairly late self-portrait of the artist. He hunted down this on the wall, and studied it. The painting, he had to admit, was a finely objective performance.

30

The clean-shaven features of the young artist were attractive, their suggestions of aesthetic sensibility being set off by a complexion which seemed whipped by wind and bronzed by sun. At the same time there was something in the expression that hinted an inner uncertainty or confusion. There had probably been a good deal that was genuinely wild and bold about Sebastian Holme. There had probably been a good deal that was simply muddled or chaotic.

Cheel frowned. In these reflections he had got his tenses wrong. *Sebastian Holme was alive.* It was odd how this one essential fact kept slipping away from him.

He moved along the line until he came to the portrait of the bearded man in front of which he had first spotted the (bearded and living) painter. Yes – shave *this* portrait and you would pretty well have the *other* portrait. But not quite. No – not *quite.* Cheel consulted his catalogue as to the painting now in front of him. It read:

> *Portrait of the Artist's Brother Gregory.*
> *Lent by Gregory Holme Esq.*

It was precisely what one might expect. Nevertheless for a moment Cheel's faith faltered. There was such plausibility in the supposition that Gregory Holme would reasonably come to the private view of his dead brother's surviving work. There was such plausibility, too, in the supposition that he would pause before the portrait his brother had painted of him, and which he had himself loaned to the show. But no! *For there had been that scar.* It *HAD* been Sebastian Holme, studying the portrait he had once painted of Gregory.

'I think I'll have a word with *you.*'

Cheel turned round in alarm – for this announcement had been made by a female voice he dimly identified, and had been spoken, moreover, in a kind of threatening hiss in his ear. Now he took one look, and his alarm turned to panic. He had been addressed by the young woman whose posterior charms had led him into that mild impropriety half an hour ago. And she was still carrying those dangerous gloves. Observing these, Cheel backed away. This horrible person had either continued to lurk around the exhibition, nursing the pleasure of a further sadistic assault upon him, or her pathological condition was such that she had actually obeyed an overwhelming impulse to return for the same purpose. To Cheel, to whom the thought of any species of physical violence was peculiarly abhorrent, this was a quite revolting circumstance.

'Isn't your name Cheel?' the young woman asked. She made the name sound as if it were an objectively displeasing one.

'I am Mervyn Cheel,' Cheel managed to say. Commonly he would have contrived to lend these words the effect of a modest but firm claim, so that the further words 'the distinguished critic and painter' would be present in a species of invisible parenthesis. On this occasion, however, he was conscious that his tone carried only the suggestion of a small-time crook making a dispirited admission to a policeman. It was not merely that his first exchange (if it could be called that) with this person had been such as to put him at a certain permanent disadvantage with her; it was also that there was something inherently alarming in the woman. This was hard to explain, but Cheel felt it acutely. 'Mervyn Cheel,' he heard himself repeating – feebly and to no purpose.

'What do you know!'

This rejoinder, which Cheel understood to be an idiom expressive of admiring surprise, was clearly being ironically used on the present occasion. It conveyed, too, the further displeasing inference that this nasty person must be of transatlantic origin. You were never really safe, Cheel reflected, with an American woman – particularly after you had pinched her bottom. He must extricate himself from this outrageously impertinent intrusion upon his privacy at once.

'Madam,' he said, taking a kind of bold scramble in the direction of dignity, 'I hardly think our acquaintance –'

'Cut it out, Cheel.' The woman was gently swinging her gloves in front of what might, in other circumstances, have been pleasing

32

contours on the upper part of her person. 'I've figured this out – see? I've heard about you. And right now I've seen you muttering with that smart cookie Braunkopf. And don't I know there's been something phoney about the whole thing? Hell I do, Mr Mervyn Cheel.'

'I'm afraid I quite fail to understand you.' Cheel's alarm and distaste were suddenly tinctured with a dawning curiosity. The woman appeared to cherish the extraordinary notion that he was involved in some sort of conspiracy with the proprietor of the Da Vinci Gallery. Her delusion was perhaps worth investigating. 'May I ask,' he said, 'who *you* are?'

'Sure,' the woman said. 'Sure you may – if you want to kid me Braunkopf hasn't told you. I'm Hedda Holme.' Her gloves swept upwards, so that Cheel sidestepped smartly. But the woman had intended only a gesture at the line of paintings behind her. 'Portrait of the Artist's Widow. That's me.'

6

She could only have been called Hedda – it occurred to Cheel – after the violently displeasing person in Ibsen's rotten old play. This might be held to testify to remarkable prescience on the part of her parents. It further suggested that these same parents had owned some shadow of literacy. Hedda's mother had perhaps been the daughter of a genuine Ibsen-vintage New Woman – something like that. How Sebastian Holme – who presumably owned such limited rationality as painters ever possess – could have come to marry the creature was wholly unclear. Or rather – Cheel suddenly saw – it wasn't. For not only was Hedda Holme, regarded *a tergo*, remarkably pinchable; she was also (although this made a less lively impression upon him personally) undeniably attractive when viewed the other way on.

He had noticed (now he came to think of it) a portrait here in the exhibition in which Holme had done justice to this female's features. Her claim to be Mrs Holme must therefore be accepted as genuine. Cheel began to wonder just when husband and wife had become – as the imbecile Braunkopf expressed it – deranged. And he began to wonder what the woman was up to now. Did she know that her husband was alive? Did she know that he had been virtually rubbing shoulders with her not half an hour ago? A somewhat oppressive sense of the obscurity of the situation with which he had become implicated momentarily discouraged Cheel. But he recovered quickly. For he had an increasingly strong sense – it might have been called intuitive, or even mystical – that *there was something in this for him*.

Meanwhile, there was the fact that Mrs Holme had introduced herself. He resented this, since he deplored any irregularity of approach between strangers. It would be best to signalize the fact at once.

'How do you do,' he said austerely.

Hedda Holme laughed shortly. At the same time her right hand, which was now resting rather inelegantly on her right hip, moved down the curve of her right buttock. It was clear that she still had it in for him as the perpetrator of that innocent little *jeu d'esprit*.

'We're going to talk,' she said. 'But not here.' She had been glancing round the Da Vinci, in which there were comparatively few people left. Now she looked appraisingly at Cheel. 'In fact I'll do you a square meal,' she added unexpectedly. With a peremptory jerk of her head, she moved away.

Cheel couldn't very well pretend to be gratified. Some such additional words as 'you hungry-looking bastard' or even 'you mangy cur' might safely have been used at this point by any imaginative writer concerned to give a little more fullness to Mrs Holme's speech. Nevertheless there was an undeniable immediate convenience in the woman's proposal. There was both that and the obscurer but equally beguiling prospect of somehow getting in on the velvet in a large way. Cheel found that he was following along. As he did so he spoke with easy dignity in the direction of the nape of Hedda Holme's neck.

34

'Let me see,' he said. 'You might care for the Caprice. Or a cab would take us to Pipistrello's in no time. Or perhaps –'

'Across the street.' The brutal woman spoke without turning round. 'There's a joint with a buffet set-up at the back. They'll fix you as much as you can eat, I guess. Tank yourself up as well, if you want to. So long as you talk, that is. And talk you will. Get, Cheel?'

For the moment, Cheel said no more. It was perhaps this form of address that chiefly offended him, and he judged silence to be the best rebuke. At the same time he remembered that his earlier reconnaissance had determined the establishment over the way as reputable and indeed promising. It ought to be possible to begin with some tolerable smoked salmon. When Mrs Holme quickened her pace, he quickened his too.

'And first,' she said, 'don't think that I don't *know*.' Occasionally sipping from a large and nauseous draught of orange juice, and alternately poking round in the dismal sort of salad that has nothing whatever to eat in it, Hedda Holme had been watching sardonically as he did civilized justice to a very tolerable *homard thermidor*. 'About the Nicolaes de Staël, that is. Most everybody does know, I guess.'

Cheel frowned. Everybody didn't know, and he wondered just how Sebastian Holme's widow did. In matters of artistic concern she must be not without an ear to the ground. The de Staël affair had been unfortunate, although of course nothing more was involved than a small chronological blunder. He wasn't too good, he had to admit, on what you might call the Lives – and Deaths – of the Painters. His vagueness about Holme was an instance. And certainly he had claimed with some confidence to have conversed with de Staël about, and in the presence of, a picture by de Staël quite a few years after de Staël turned out to have died. As this venially inaccurate recollection had been advanced in the course of making a professional *expertise*, and as the resulting attribution to de Staël had happened to bring him in a reasonable fee, a certain unpleasantness had naturally succeeded upon the discovery of the truth of the matter. But it wasn't true that *everybody* knew. If they did, his present position would be even more unjustly depressed than it was. Not even the wretched provincial rag might be employing him.

'Ah, that,' he said whimsically. 'There has been a certain amount of uninformed gossip about it. The true facts are rather amusing and quite innocent. Unfortunately I'm not at liberty to divulge them at present.'

'You're a crook, Cheel, and you know it. In the picture-broking racket you've brought off some very pretty swindles in your time. So has that rogue Braunkopf. And there were the two of you, muttering to each other in the middle of the bastard's paintings –'

'The bastard?' For the moment Cheel was simply unable to decide at what point of the woman's raving he was most flabbergasted.

'Sure, Cheel. The low hound I married. And there you and Braunkopf were, conspiring together. I mean to get to the bottom of it.'

The woman must be in some advanced stage of paranoia. Cheel felt extremely annoyed. He resented the suggestion that he was in the habit of bringing off successful swindles in the picture-broking world. It was something that he had just never got in on. The melancholy de Staël affair was an instance of his total failure, to date, in anything of the sort. He didn't even believe that Braunkopf was really in any notable degree a rogue. Hedda Holme was one hundred per cent crazy.

'Forty per cent,' Hedda Holme said – so that Cheel positively jumped. 'Shall I tell you how Braunkopf tricked me into agreeing to a commission like that? Swearing the slob's daubs were the next thing to junk, and that it would cost the earth to start a legend about him.'

'A legend?'

'All that hocum about Wamba-Wamba. A cover story, if ever there was one.'

'You mean that all that never happened? You mean that your husband's still alive?' This last question escaped Cheel's lips simply because he was by now thoroughly dazed. As it turned out, he could scarcely have asked a better one.

'Alive? You're crazy. Sebastian's dead, all right. That's the one bright spot in the affair. Why –'

'Yes, of course.' Cheel interrupted. For Sebastian Holme's supposed widow had spoken with spontaneous and complete conviction. Whatever her suspicions were, he, Cheel, was one ahead of her in a crucial piece of knowledge. 'But what do you mean,' he demanded, 'by hocum at Wamba-Wamba?'

'That's what *you* know. You and your fellow-crook Braunkopf. So where are all those paintings? That's what *I* want to discover.'

'You mean the paintings destroyed by the mob, or whatever it was, in this outlandish Wamba place? Dust and ashes, I suppose, blowing through the jungle.'

'Are you kidding?' Mrs Holme put her heaviest irony into this question. 'Braunkopf has them. And you're in on it.'

'Don't I damned well wish I was.' Cheel was about to add 'you silly bitch' (or perhaps merely 'you stupid cow') to this avowal. But he desisted, perhaps feeling that he had produced sufficient candour for one mouthful. Instead, he decided to try sounding a rational note. 'Have some sense,' he said. 'Braunkopf may have shot you a line about the cost of building up the Wamba affair. But he couldn't have intended it, you know – whether to grab a lot of pictures, as you seem to suggest, or simply to create a legend. Mind you, he *has* created a legend. The success of this exhibition has a silly side which is certainly bound up with that. By the way, I suppose you realize that, legend or no legend, your husband – your *late* husband – could paint?'

'Of course he could paint. Somebody must have taught him, I suppose. He produced acres of the stuff.'

'You imbecile bitch! Sebastian Holme could *paint*.' Cheel was heartily glad that he had saved up his imprecation for this point. For the first time, Hedda Holme seemed a trifle shaken. 'Do you know what that means? Of course you don't. But what you do know is that you're sitting bloody pretty on this whole business.

Even at sixty per cent, it means tens of thousands for you. So lay off your crackpot suspicions. All that stuff in the catalogue – their stupid revolution, and the burning of some rotten hotel – must be on the record, you know. The notion that this little Braunkopf creature somehow rigged it in order to steal the pictures of a painter who still wasn't worth twopence just won't wash, my girl. It's as potty as your notion that I was in on it too. How's your salad? Useful for keeping down the *embonpoint*, I suppose. They're not too bad with lobsters here. They can bring me my *tournedos* now.' Cheel raised his wine-glass amiably and chinked it against the tumbler containing his hostess's orange juice. He remembered the corpulent man in the Da Vinci. 'Cheers,' he said.

Mrs Holme quite failed to respond to this civility.

'I've been swindled,' she said. 'And I've a hunch you're in on it.' She looked at Cheel balefully but (he thought) a shade uncertainly. Perhaps she was coming to some glimmering perception of her own fatuity. 'Braunkopf and you have gotten all those African paintings – the ones there's this phoney story about – and you're going to unload them quietly and slowly on the market.'

'I see,' Cheel said. He found himself speaking almost respectfully. It was a nice thought, after all – so nice that he couldn't do other than mourn its baselessness. 'You think the show the catalogue speaks about in this Wamba Palace Hotel never took place at all?'

'It took place, all right. There was a printed catalogue of that one too. I possess a copy of it.'

'Well then – there you are.' This time, Cheel spoke almost absently. For, with Hedda Holme's last remark, something had started up in his mind like a creation. As yet, like all great imaginative constructions at their moment of birth, the thing was unformed and shadowy. *But it was there.* Cheel took a long draught of claret. 'And so what?' he asked.

'I don't believe for a moment that they were destroyed.' Mrs Holme bit viciously into the plainly nauseous fluff of a starch-reduced roll. 'Certainly not all of them. Probably not any of them.

38

Somebody just walked off with them in the confusion. Or perhaps bought them up at a dollar a piece.'

'It's an interesting notion.' Cheel found that he wanted to laugh rudely. He did so. 'Has it occurred to you that if they *were* saved, and *were* bought up at a dollar a piece, you yourself wouldn't preserve the slightest title or interest in them?'

'A sale like that would be a fraud, a racket.'

'My good woman, masterpieces have changed hands before now for no more than the price of –' Cheel was about to add 'a square meal' but changed this, on second thoughts, to 'a packet of cigarettes.' 'And such a deal,' he went on, 'would be perfectly valid, if freely entered into. Even if some of your husband's paintings turned up after having simply disappeared, you wouldn't find it easy to break in on any subsequent transaction and establish a claim to them. Ask your lawyer – your attorney, I should say.'

'I don't believe it. It wouldn't be just.'

'Well, the situation simply isn't going to arise, so we shall never know. If you had any sense, you'd be content with what you've got. If you own all that stuff over the road – and I suppose you do – then you're damned lucky. Your husband might have made a will, leaving it all elsewhere. He might have divorced you, which would have been pretty rational.' Cheel thought of adding: 'Or he might have drowned you in your bath, which would have been more rational still.' Fear of a further vulgar physical assault, however, restrained him. 'Perhaps just a morsel of Stilton,' he said instead. 'And a drop of brandy with the coffee.'

The meal wore pleasantly to its close. What Cheel asked for, that is to say, was set before him. He ceased much to bother his head about Mrs Holme. Temporarily, at least – and he hoped for good – her bolt was shot. It had been a bolt sufficiently blindly directed in the first place, and she was obviously a person of low intelligence. It was true that there remained a certain element of the enigmatic about her. The terms in which she addressed him had been almost uniformly offensive – and this had, of course, displeased one of Cheel's breeding and sensibilities very much. On the other hand, she had come clean with this entirely satisfactory repast. No doubt there had been some notion of simple bribery in her head. Having formed – more or less at the drop of a handkerchief – the fantastic idea that he was in league with Braunkopf, she had capped it by supposing that he could be detached from a lucrative swindle by a mingling of opprobrious speech with cakes and ale. This mis-estimate of his quality, if comical, was annoying. Nevertheless Cheel now found himself in a mood of considerable post-prandial contentment. He had lunched without spending a penny after all. And meanwhile – what was far more important – his vision had come to him. He thought of the poet Keats, on tiptoe to explore the vastness of his first long poem. He thought of Mrs Holme's compatriot Henry James at the moment of its dawning on him that *The Golden Bowl*, say, was to be a work of some complexity. Yes, he felt rather like that.

So now he must get away and think. He watched with satisfaction as Hedda Holme paid quite a large bill. She wasn't, in a sense, getting any change out of it, either. She was gathering up her bag and those damned gloves. Cheel glanced round the little restaurant. It was better appointed than one would expect, simply glancing in from the bar which had represented his first interest in the place. You had to go through the bar to reach the exit – and then, of course, immediately opposite, was the Da Vinci Gallery. He was still interested in the bar. If he were to succeed in contacting Sebastian Holme again (and this was now imperative) he would have to put into execution the plan he had already formed. He would have to put in time in a chair by a window, with his eye on the entrance to Braunkopf's establishment.

Mervyn Cheel had just reminded himself of this when he suddenly became aware that events had, so to speak, got ahead of him. In the bar, so far as he could command it from his present position, there was no longer any sort of lunch-hour crush. In fact there were only three customers to be seen. Two of them, confabulating together while perched on stools and drinking gin-and-tonics, might be motor-salesmen, or persons of that rank of life. This, indeed, was only a conjecture. But the identity of the third man, who was sitting hard by the door, admitted no doubt whatever. He was – once more, beard and all – the late Sebastian Holme.

7

Strictly speaking, there ought not to have been anything unexpected in this turn of events. It was as natural (or unnatural) that the late Holme should hover in the vicinity of his pictures as that the Ghost of Hamlet's Father should perambulate the battlements of Elsinore. And as the Da Vinci must be a place of hazard to one in Holme's peculiar position it was equally natural that, before essaying a further foray there, he should pause to fortify himself in this conveniently located hostelry.

Cheel was taken unawares, all the same. It is therefore to his credit that he saw at once the need for decisive action. Whether Sebastian Holme had spotted his wife in the Da Vinci earlier that morning was something Cheel couldn't be sure of. It seemed probable that he had, since he must certainly have reckoned on her being present there. Presuming that he was anxious to continue unrecognized, as surely he must, then his turning up at all on such an occasion seemed to argue a rashness in temperament that Cheel felt it might be useful to register. However all this might be, it did seem certain that Hedda Holme hadn't, in her turn, spotted her husband. Perhaps her glance hadn't fallen upon him at all. Perhaps it had, and she had taken him for her brother-in-law Gregory Holme, whom for some reason she had chosen to ignore. Perhaps the bearded figure had conveyed nothing at all to her. It would be odd, of course, if she had failed to penetrate a disguise which had been instantly patent to Cheel. But then she was a singularly stupid woman – whereas he, Cheel, was a quite exceptionally intelligent man.

It was intelligence that was needed now. If Mrs Holme had stared unregardingly at Mr Holme once, this didn't at all mean that she would do so a second time. And there was no question of her not even noticing the man. In order to reach the street she would have to pass within a couple of feet of him. And Cheel, although still so much in the dark as to the inwardness of the situation he had stumbled upon, was very sure that his scope for profitable manoeuvre in the face of it would be sadly straitened should the painter forthwith be restored – whether willingly or unwillingly – to the embrace of his not particularly sorrowful widow. He had to prevent the risk of an encounter. And he had seconds in which to manage it.

For Hedda Holme was on her feet. As he scrambled out of his own chair (for his problem had made him a little tardy in the exercise of his accustomed good manners), she turned away from him and began to thread her way among the tables towards the bar. She couldn't herself, at the moment, either see Sebastian Holme or be seen by him. But the breathing-space thus afforded was only fractional – and Cheel was doing no better than follow helplessly in Hedda's wake. Then something came to his aid. It was no more than a start of memory: one occasioned by their relative postures as they moved. *There it was*: swaying, tightly skirted, delightfully challenging in its own right. Cheel put out his hand and pinched.

This time, he pinched so hard that Hedda gave a loud yell. It was a sound that came like music to his ear, and he managed to stand his ground with a very tolerable stoicism as she whirled round on him. But the strength of her punch to his jaw surprised him, so that he quite genuinely staggered and toppled, and had little difficulty in making a thoroughly verisimilar business of upsetting a whole laden table as he fell.

Not unnaturally, pandemonium broke loose. The little disturbance in the Da Vinci had been no more than a mere murmuring in the comparison. The majority of the remaining lunchers rose hastily, knocking over their chairs, spilling their coffee, and retreating with precipitation to the sides of the room.

Hedda, unfortunately, was not retreating; with a resourcefulness he could only admire, she had equipped herself with an ugly-looking weapon probably designed for the dissection of cold ham and was again advancing upon him rapidly. Hell, he reflected as he dodged, hath no fury like a woman pinched quite as hard as that. Hedda was also shouting. She was accusing him (he gathered as he dodged round a potted palm) not of sadism or indecency but of base ingratitude. It was true that she did have some small reason to be surprised. And so would anyone (he had grasped this crucial fact) who heard her plaint. What had just happened, although in certain situations (in a tube train, for instance, or even in a crowded picture gallery) it entertainingly *does* happen, precisely does *not* happen as a gentleman follows a lady with whom he has been quietly lunching in a respectable restaurant. Poor Hedda was plainly off her rocker.

The shindy must, of course, abundantly have reached the little bar between the restaurant and the street. Both Sebastian Holme and the motor-salesmen would have been moved to take a peep in at it – and by this time Holme, having spotted Hedda, would certainly have made himself scarce. The crisis was over. Or it would be over as soon as he had successfully terminated the little fracas he was now involved with. For one of a sedentary habit Cheel was fortunately possessed of a very creditable degree of mobility. Evasive action afforded him no difficulty. At this moment, for instance, a couple of agile side-steps sufficed to interpose between Hedda and himself the person of an elderly and apparently infirm woman who could only hobble with the aid of a stick.

'I'm terribly sorry,' Cheel murmured as he dodged her. 'My wife is liable to these delusional states. But nobody is in any danger except myself.' He gave the infirm woman a dexterous shove further into Hedda's path, and was thereby enabled to gain the more secure shelter of an able-bodied waiter. 'Get it away from her,' he said.

The waiter – perhaps surprisingly – did just as he was told; he stepped up to the panting Hedda and took the carving-knife

43

from her hand. He was joined by a woman who looked as if she might preside over a cloak-room, and who appeared to have a professional line in soothing noises for occasions like this. Near the door, another waiter was restraining a junior colleague, who had rashly thought to rush outside and shout for the police. Several guests were calling frigidly for their bills. And a flabby man, who was certainly the manager, was approaching Cheel with a forbidding but at the same time wary expression. Cheel took the initiative at once.

'Sorry about this,' he said, politely but with a touch of *hauteur*. 'Fact is, it's weeks since my wife had one of these turns, and I thought lunch out might buck her up. But it hasn't answered, as you see. Have them call a cab, please. My car's not due back for half an hour. Send me a bill, of course, for any damage. Lord Basset. Two esses, one tee. Send it to me at the House of Lords.'

The manager gave a nod to the waiter near the door, and Cheel was heartened to hear a taxi being whistled up. At the same time he became aware that one of the guests – clearly a motor-salesman superior in the hierarchy to the two who had been drinking at the bar – had thrust himself forward in grossly vulgar curiosity. Cheel turned to him.

'See you're a physician,' he murmured. 'Professional interest, eh? Distressing thing. Sporadic delusions, you know.' He lowered his voice. 'Fantasies of petty sexual assault, and so on. Her time of life, you know.' He turned to Hedda – who, he was delighted to see, was now reduced to weeping quietly. 'That's right, Ianthe?' he said more loudly. 'Your time of life, eh? Cheer up, old girl. No harm done.'

He moved confidently towards the door. The first waiter and the cloak-room woman continued to flank Hedda, urging and assisting her forward. The manager, hovering in front, spoke for the first time.

'We are most extremely sorry,' he said in a loud voice, and plainly for the benefit of any of his patrons who cared to listen. 'Extremely sorry, my lord, that her ladyship has been taken ill.' He made Cheel a low bow, and at the same time gave him a glance of extreme malevolence. It was obvious that he had no more belief in this disastrous guest as Lord Basset (with however many tees and esses) than he had in him as the Grand Cham of Tartary. 'Get out,' he hissed in Cheel's ear. 'Try that once again and I'll have you put where you belong. Inside, see?' He made another low bow. '*Good* afternoon, my lady. A happier occasion, I hope. Old and valued clients. Most distressed.' He waved imperiously to a waiter to open the door.

They were on the pavement. Cheel's satisfaction in his conduct of the episode was only slightly marred by the realization that (as so frequently happened) his moral character had been shockingly aspersed. It was the manager's notion that the affair had been no more than a low put-up job, contrived between this revolting woman and himself in the interest of getting away with a free meal. Cheel glanced with distaste at Hedda – and it struck him that there was no time to lose. At any moment she might recover her accustomed nervous tone and take another swipe at him. Hastily he assisted in shoving her through the open door of the taxi – and then closed it on her with a bang.

'Where to, sir?' The driver, seeing that there was to be only one passenger, was leaning inquiringly out of his little glass compartment.

'Holloway Gaol,' Cheel hissed in his ear. 'Main entrance.' He pressed a pound note into the man's hand and stood back. Watching the taxi drive off, he handed the waiter and the cloak-room woman a half-crown apiece. His lunch had cost him something, after all. He was well satisfied, all the same. He glanced at his watch, and was surprised at the time. But then – as was remarked by a Shakespearean character whom he greatly admired – pleasure and action make the hours seem short.

8

The afternoon was fine, and he decided to take a turn in the mild London sunshine. His living quarters, as it happened, were not at the present time commodious, and spaciousness was in consequence a sensation that he had to seek *en plein air*. On this occasion he decided for St James's Park. It had frequently – he remembered – proved particularly propitious for the smooth functioning of his intellectual faculties. He was inclined, indeed, to indulge the fancy that, at either end, its vistas closed at precisely the distance most congenial to what might be called the range of his own mind. Moreover the route thither was not without sundry associative and nostalgic charms. He would pass a club from which, through a misunderstanding, he had been obliged to resign some years before, but for which he preserved nevertheless (such was the refinement of his spirit) a benign and wholly unresentful regard. He would pass another club which – again because of a stupid misunderstanding – had a couple of years later simply refused to let him in. The incident saved him a certain amount of money that he hadn't possessed. Finally he would cross the Mall. There, of course, Royalty might drive by – and Royalty so utterly royal that it would be proper to halt and turn respectfully roadwards as one swept off one's hat. Mervyn Cheel, who was eminently well-affected to the Crown, could rely upon an encounter like this to make his day.

The Mall, in fact, was void. St James's Park, on the other hand was crowded enough – and in the main with persons demonstrably from the simpler classes of society. Cheel found nothing disagreeable about this, since his social tolerance was such that the spectacle of his inferiors always held something gratifying to him. He did however draw the line at sharing a bench with a prole, and his fastidiousness for a time made it difficult to call a halt to his perambulation and seat himself in meditative ease. This, since he had a good deal to meditate, was vexatious, and he was glad when he did eventually find an unencumbered resting place. It was in full sunshine, and Buckingham Palace (always referred to by Cheel as Buck House) was cheerfully in view, with the Royal Standard flying above its roof. Cheel felt as pleased by this token of the sovereign presence as if it had been a private signal instructing him to drop in there for a drink.

But – he told himself – to work! His encounter with Hedda Holme had not – at least in any clearly analysable terms – brought him very much. Yet it had been abundantly worth while, since it *had* brought him that moment of cloudy but indubitable inspiration. How was he to clarify this? Not perhaps by taking, here and now, too anxious thought about the affair. For the higher reaches of imaginative achievement were, after all, intuitive territory. He would do best to cultivate a wise passiveness; to expose his mind, vacant and unemployed, to some seminal percolation from its own abundant inner recesses.

Coming down Piccadilly, he had bought an early edition of some evening paper. Pursuing his design of mental relaxation, he opened it and idly scanned its columns. There was, he found – as was to be expected – a notice of the Holme exhibition at the Da Vinci. Needless to say, it was a grossly incompetent affair – but at least the scribbler had caught the trick of shouting with what was going to be the crowd. It was what journalists call a rave notice. He read it through, and found himself wondering whether Sebastian Holme himself had read it yet. He too might have bought a copy of the paper in Piccadilly – if indeed he hadn't been too discomposed at having in such odd circumstances just avoided his wife only an hour ago.

What was Holme doing now? What had he been doing yesterday, and what would he be doing tomorrow?

As Cheel asked himself these questions he felt a faint tingling down the length of his spine. They were unremarkable questions, in a loose or quasi-logical concatenation, and must be called ruminative or even wool-gathering rather than of any evident penetration. Yet Cheel saw instantly that they drove to the heart of the matter. For the answer to all of them was: *Damn all*. Or perhaps: *Eating his bloody head off*. For purposes of more elegant expression it might be said that Holme was (in that phrase of Henry James's for a nicely poised character) *en disponibilité*. The silly sod (and this had been Cheel's grand, glimmering perception from the first) was crying out to be *used*. In a sense this was true of all human beings. It was what they were there for, and success in life was a matter of being always on the job. But Sebastian Holme's was a very special case. It had every title to call itself a challenging case. And the challenge was one to which any man in whom there breathed the spirit of true enterprise must feel virtually a moral compulsion to respond.

By such Enterprise – Cheel recalled the poet Spenser as declaring – *many rich Regions are discovered*. But that – he reflected, as he gazed once more at his sovereign's flag flying over her palace – had been in the First Elizabethan Age. There was far too little bold and resolute seizing of opportunity in the Second. People no longer, like Drake and Raleigh and worthies of that kidney, went out after things. Britons had become degenerate. They just didn't know when and how to grab. In his own present situation nine out of ten of his countrymen would be perfectly content to do nothing at all. Cheel felt himself blushing for them.

But just *what* was to be done? First, he must track down Sebastian Holme once more. Holme must then be roused from his culpable skulking and idling, his reprehensible inutility. Whatever his motive for being dead, he must be brought alive again. Or rather, he must be brought, so to speak, half-alive. Yes – that was precisely it. And it must all be done by kindness – unless, of course, the situation, when further explored, suggested that more could be achieved by brutality. Firmly but kindly for a start, the young man must be shown how he ought to be comporting himself.

Cheel leant back on his bench, enjoying a relaxation promoted alike by the sunshine and the consciousness of his own benevolence. The movement made him aware that he was no longer alone. A man had sat down next to him and was now reading a newspaper. It was the same newspaper that he had himself purchased. The man was reading something on one of the middle pages; it might quite well be the critical notice of the Sebastian Holme Exhibition. The man gave a grunt which could have been of contempt or impatience or irritation, and he then let the paper drop to his side. Cheel turned slightly away. He had no impulse to inspect an undistinguished and probably plebeian stranger. Even so, the paper was within his vision, as was the man's left hand, loosely holding it. Cheel suddenly froze. There was no mistaking that scar. He had been looking at it not much more than a couple of hours ago. In all the wide world, only Sebastian Holme had precisely *that* at the base of his left index finger and thumb.

For a moment the impression was overwhelming. Cheel was less conscious of the fantastic coincidence that had once more brought his quarry (which was perhaps the word) within his reach than he was of what a psychologist would have termed a purely ideated image. He saw once more the silly little screaming girl; he felt the bottle splinter as he swung it behind him; he smelt not only the reek of tobacco-smoke and alcohol but also (although this seemed fanciful) the warm blood spurting from the stupid young dauber's hand. So powerful were these recollections that he found himself actually trying to dodge the blow which, in another second, was going to lay him out.

Then all this faded. The plain fact was that he had enjoyed the most incredible luck. He turned and looked boldly at Sebastian Holme – only to give a strangled yelp of astonishment. The man with the scar on his hand was as clean-shaven as he himself.

9

Or more so. It was when he noted this – the almost unnatural smoothness of Holme's skin – and when he received too a faint whiff as of some cosmetic preparation floating in the air, that Cheel began to master the quite uncomfortable degree of bewilderment that had assailed him. Within the hour, Holme had had himself shaved.

'What have you gone and done that for?' It was with large surprise that Cheel heard himself speak with this admirable directness. He had done so out of an urgent sense that big issues were at stake.

'Gone and done what?' As he asked this, Holme's gaze narrowed. 'Aren't you that bounder Cheel?'

'Yes.' It would have been more accordant with dignity, perhaps, to qualify this reply. But Cheel was bent on business. 'Gone and had your beard off.'

'Not my beard. Somebody else's.'

'I know. Your brother Gregory's.'

'How the hell do you know that?'

'Portrait of the Artist's Brother Gregory. Lent by Gregory Holme Esq.'

'Of course.' Holme stared gloomily at Cheel. Then he seemed to remember. 'What were you doing with my wife in that pub?'

'Trying to get to the bottom of something.'

'And why was there a rumpus?'

'Same reply, in a manner of speaking.' Cheel was so pleased with this witticism that he took time off for a good laugh. 'I'd pinched her behind. She resented it. Incalculable creatures, the ladies.'

'You had a nerve.' Holme was staring at Cheel with something like respect. 'She's an awful woman.'

'I know.'

'Why did you pinch her behind? For the hell of it?'

'No. I'd done that earlier, as a matter of fact – in your show.'

'In my show!' Holme was suddenly indignant. 'What do you mean, wasting your time assaulting people in my show? Why didn't you look at the pictures, and not the wenches? But you always were a filthy man. Don't I remember.'

'Yes, yes,' Cheel said. He saw no reason to linger over inessentials. 'But I pinched your wife the second time as what you might call a diversionary manoeuvre. It started a row; you peered in from the bar; and then you made off. In fact, I gave you the alarm, and I hope you're grateful. If she'd seen you she might have recognized you. I'm surprised she didn't do so in the Da Vinci. It was half-witted, by the way, going in there today if you want people to think you're dead.'

'I couldn't keep away. And the pictures shook me. I decided to go back later – and first I thought I'd have a quick one in that bar. When there was the rumpus, and I peered in and saw Hedda yelling like that – well, that shook me too.'

'And now you've shaken the beard off?'

'That's just it. You know the devil of a lot. I decided I couldn't bear it any longer.'

'Being dead?'

'Being dead.'

'I think you ought to reconsider that.' Cheel said this in a weighty and judicious manner. He didn't at all like the way the thing was going. And he looked nervously round as he spoke. St James's Park was frequented by all sorts of people, and at any moment somebody might drift along and, so to speak, welcome Holme back from the grave. 'You mustn't do anything rash. You owe it to yourself to consider the whole matter carefully. In fact I think we ought to go somewhere and discuss it in private.'

'What's this about? What the devil has it to do with you?' Although Holme was obviously in some state of muddle or bewilderment he was also irritated and indignant. 'Messing around with my wife, and now wanting to go somewhere private. You must be a sex maniac. I don't want to have anything to do with you. You're a filthy man, and I've always known it. And it's too late anyway. I'm giving myself up. That's why I blewed five bob on getting rid of the beard. It was Hedda who tipped the balance. She's an awful woman. You couldn't know how awful. But somehow she made me feel that this being dead business is a mistake. It has simply no future.'

'That's just where you may be wrong. I'd like to talk it over with you.' Cheel stole a glance at the sulky, but at the same time sensitive and vulnerable face which the disappearance of the beard had revealed. 'And that's part of the trouble with being dead and buried, I suppose. Nobody to talk the whole thing over with.'

'Perhaps it is. But I don't trust you, Cheel. Mervyn Cheel, isn't it?'

'Yes.'

'Well, there you are.'

'Don't be silly, Holme. You can't really be silly. Nobody who painted those things could be silly. It's my job. I *know*.'

'They surprised you? They surprised me. Brought together like that, and with all those nobs snapping them up. As I said, it shook me. And made me mad, as Hedda would say. Foolish, but I admit it.'

'Then let me talk to you, my dear man.'

'I'm not your dear man. And I don't want anything today. Didn't you see the notice on the gate? No Hawkers. Keep Out. This Means You.'

'Holme, don't be bitter. It's true I may have something to sell. But you'd find it a damned good buy. Only, first, I must have the facts.'

'Beware of the Dog.'

'Of course if you can *only* be silly, I must simply go away.'

'Although we abound in charity, we do not give at the door. Scram.'

52

'Very well.' Cheel got to his feet with dignity. 'My assistance is rejected. The incident is closed.'

'Fine. And when you meet a copper, send him along.'

'Here's one coming along now, as it happens. Constable!' Cheel raised a summoning hand as he spoke. But he hadn't really spoken at all loudly – a circumstance which he trusted to Holme's disturbed condition to obscure from him. And this worked.

'No – stop!' Holme made an agitated grab at his companion. 'I've got to think. I don't know that I mean it – about giving myself up.'

'Precisely.' Cheel sat down again with the same poise with which he had risen. The policeman went past with no more than a glance at the man who had appeared to gesture a little oddly. 'Precisely,' Cheel repeated. 'As you say, we've got to think out this thing together. And first – once again – the facts. Just what will you be in for, if they catch you?'

'I don't quite know. I've never seen it happen. Once or twice I heard it in the distance. They say it can last about a week.'

'I see.' Cheel, of course, didn't at all see – unless it was the sudden possibility of Sebastian Holme's being mad. 'It has to do with your brother Gregory, I suppose?'

'Yes, it does in a way have to do with him.'

'Did you kill him?'

'Kill Gregory?' Sebastian Holme stared at Cheel in unfeigned astonishment. 'Of course not. Rather the opposite, really. You might say I've brought him alive.'

'You are *being* Gregory now – or, at least, you *were* being until you shaved off the beard this afternoon?'

'That's pretty obvious, isn't it?'

'And Gregory is, in fact, dead?'

'Obvious again. Gregory's dead. Beastly dead. I liked him very much.' Holme paused for a moment, and Cheel was revolted to notice that the young man had tears in his eyes.

'*His* body became *me* dead. I became *him* alive. It seemed the simplest thing.'

53

'This was during the revolution, or whatever it was, in this outlandish Wamba place?'

'Of course.'

'Where things weren't at all as they seemed. You weren't killed. Perhaps your paintings weren't destroyed?'

'Not destroyed?' Holme seemed astonished again. 'Of course they were destroyed. I saw it happen with my own eyes. I can tell you it's a very nasty thing to see. Almost as nasty as seeing –' Holme checked himself. 'Not destroyed!' he repeated with contempt. 'What put that in your head?'

'It's a notion of your wife's. She thinks they were saved and somehow collared by Braunkopf. She thinks Braunkopf's holding on to them until your reputation's at its peak. Then he'll unload them quietly for the benefit of his own pocket.'

'What ghastly tripe.'

'No doubt. Your wife does strike me as a suspecting sort.'

'She's an awful woman. You might get on with her rather well. She might even come to tolerate your dirty little tricks. It's an idea. Horrible Hedda and her heel Cheel.'

A man unequipped with Mervyn Cheel's natural magnanimity might have resented this. It did, indeed, produce a moment's silence. But Cheel could afford not to feel offended. He was pretty sure that he had as good as got Sebastian Holme where he wanted him. Of course there was much that still had to be found out before a master-plan could evolve itself. But the essence of the situation was now clear.

In one regard, however, Cheel recognized (with his usual penetration) that he had some little way to go. Holme's last remark might be said to emphasize this. If the situation now unfolding satisfactorily were to be successfully exploited (not that 'exploited' would be the word to employ) then something of an honest and wholesome relation of confidence must be built up with this obviously kittle and difficult young man. Holme must not simply follow along; he must eat out of the hand. Cheel must be not merely manager and impresario; he must be guardian angel as well. Holme must come – and that quickly – to bless the hour at which he had sat down on this particular bench in St James's Park. It could hardly be denied that, before this could be achieved, there was a certain amount of existing prejudice to overcome. Holme, unfortunately, carried one occasion of this prejudice about with him under his thumb. Literally that. The problem of getting him – this time metaphorically – under *Cheel's* thumb was a little complicated by the fact.

'There's an impersonal side to this,' Cheel said. 'And it's what chiefly makes me want to help. Mind you, I want to do that simply as a matter of man to man. You must know very well what it is to be liked, because you're a very likeable person. Although it can't be said that you've been exactly cordial this afternoon, I do myself happen to like you simply as a chap.'

'I didn't have any lunch,' Holme said. 'Otherwise, this is where I'd vomit.'

'But it's something else I'm talking about.' Cheel pursued his way determinedly. 'What I've called the impersonal side. The business, I mean, of getting you back to your painting. Or perhaps you *are* back at it? If so, I'm talking to no purpose.'

'Cut it out. Look at me, Cheel. Look at me sitting in this rotten place and putting in time talking to a blackguard. Of course I'm not back to painting.'

'So I'd have supposed.' Although Holme's remarks were still a little lacking in expression of regard, Cheel felt satisfied with the turn the talk was taking. It was bringing into Holme's eye a glint he wanted to see there. 'And my point is, you know, that it's a plain duty to get you back into a studio. You're a youngster still, if you'll forgive my mentioning the fact, and moreover quite a bit of your mature production went west in that stupid hotel. *There just must be more Sebastian Holmes.* Put it that I feel the thing professionally. As it happens, I've painted a little myself.' Cheel was disingenuously modest. 'I still do from time to time, although I've no illusions about the extent of my talent.'

'Illustrations for smutty books – or just designs for chocolate boxes?'

'Small pointillist abstracts.' Cheel now hardly noticed Holme's continued offensiveness. His instinct told him that the moment of crisis had come. 'In the main, of course, I'm just a critic – a sterile intellectual. But the fact that I *do* a little myself – '

'Yes, of course.' Holme's impatience was suddenly of a new sort. 'Get on, can't you?'

'A man with your gift owes a duty to it. That's the plain fact of the matter, Holme. It's your business to paint. So why aren't you painting?'

There was a silence. Holme – and it was for the first time – seemed to have decided that Cheel had advanced something worth thinking about.

'That's interesting,' Holme said. 'It's interesting because there's no creditable answer. No honest answer I wouldn't be a bit ashamed to give. And yet I haven't quite seen it that way. Thanks.'

'You've got some money, I suppose?'

'Damned little. But I've got some.'

'You could hire an attic, buy a canvas or two, and get down to work? And you don't feel you've exhausted your inspiration?'

'Inspiration my foot. I'm a painter and that's that.' Holme was now looking bewildered. 'It's true I could do these things. And true that I don't seem to want to. It must be connected with this change of identity. *I was* the painter – not Gregory.'

'I think you're on to something there.' Cheel nodded approvingly, as at an apt pupil's first steps to comprehension. 'You have to get back to free artistic expression in your own essential character.' Cheel had made this sound quite impressive, and for a moment he paused on it weightily. 'Or at least,' he added as an afterthought, '*almost* free artistic expression.'

'You think something can be done?' Holme's voice had become frankly appealing. At the same time he looked round apprehensively. 'It was damned silly of me to take off the beard. Anybody might come along.'

'That's what I've been thinking.'

'Or Hedda might. She's a perfectly awful woman, you know. She might do absolutely anything. She might call a policeman.'

'We certainly don't want anything like that.' Holme, Cheel saw, was a reformed character. At least he was that for the moment – for he seemed to be a young man subject to somewhat rapid changes of mood. Doubtless he might turn sulky again – and in consequence thoroughly rude – at any moment. It would be prudent in Cheel to press hard upon the initiative he now held. 'And we need privacy in any case. There's much to get clear. I must have the full facts, you know. That's only fair.'

'Yes, I suppose so.' Holme sounded reluctant. 'But it's such a horrid story. There are parts of it I just don't like remembering at all.'

'You must get it off your chest.' Cheel said this in a manly and encouraging way, like a schoolmaster keeping eventual disciplinary intentions out of sight. 'We'll go to my rooms. It's about time for a cup of tea. Come along, my dear chap.'

'I'm not your –' Quite pathetically, Sebastian Holme checked himself. 'All right,' he said. 'I'll come.'

10

'Of course these aren't my regular quarters,' Cheel said twenty minutes later. 'The fact is my flat's being decorated, and I've moved in here to be out of the mess.'

'What rot!' Holme, who was prowling round the room, spoke contemptuously. He appeared to have gone into opposition again. 'It's clear enough that you're in pretty low water. A sleazy character in seedy circumstances. That's you. You needn't be ashamed of it. At any rate, not of the circumstances.' He moved to the window and inspected it. 'You've got a damned good north light. A man could paint ten hours a day here, if he wanted to. I don't expect you last out as long as that. But let me see some of the pointillist things you were talking about.'

'It's the application of the technique to abstractions that I've been finding interesting.' Surprised and gratified, Cheel produced some of his recent labours. 'One can't just be a critic all the time.'

'Can't one?' For some minutes Holme studied with care the small paintings shown to him. 'Yes,' he said. 'I see. You're rather a clever person, Cheel.' He turned away, suddenly indifferent. 'Which doesn't mean these things aren't pretty average rubbish. They are.'

'Thank you very much.' For the first time in the course of his exchanges with the disagreeable Sebastian Holme, Cheel was really offended. Indeed, he was deeply mortified. He managed, however, to say no more than: 'If that's settled, perhaps we can get back to business.'

'Exactly. You're broke, or the next thing to it. And honest work isn't your line. So you've decided that you can somehow cash in on having discovered me.' A quick grin came over the young man's face. 'Money from Holme. That's your notion.'

'Money *for* Holme, too.' Cheel was recovering something like good humour. It seemed to him that Holme's rather crude phrasing of the matter wasn't wholly unpromising. 'But, of course, I may have got the thing wrong. So I want the facts. In the first place, about Wamba, or Wamba-Wamba, or whatever its name is.'

'Wamba is the territory – the state, as they now call it . Wamba-Wamba is the town, or capital. The people are called the Wamba. They're terrific. Particularly in a dapple of light through jungle foliage. You just wouldn't believe what happens to their skins. There's not the minutest area that you couldn't explore for days. I'd done no more than make a beginning at that. And now I'll never be able to go near the place again.' Holme glanced up at Cheel – his mood of anxiety and incipient dependence suddenly returned to him. 'I take it your damned cleverness doesn't see a way to my doing *that*?'

'One thing at a time, my dear chap. We must walk before we can run. Now, what about your manner of living at present? To just what extent are you being your brother Gregory?'

'I collect his money from the bank, to begin with. Only they tell me there isn't much left.'

'I'm sorry to hear that.' In point of fact, Cheel found this information satisfactory. Sebastian Holme had been forging his brother's signature. Knowledge of this would be useful if the young man later turned recalcitrant. 'What else?'

'Well, I keep away from people who knew Gregory, and I skip around pretty quickly from one set of digs to another. I couldn't manage a real impersonation. And Hedda has been trying to contact me. I mean she's been trying to contact Gregory. It's all very confusing. And there's no future in it, as I said. I wouldn't have come back to England at all, if there hadn't been some stupid difficulty about drawing on Gregory's money abroad. And yet I *wanted* to come back. If I can't be in Wamba, I'd sooner be in England.'

'What sort of a person was your brother Gregory?'

'Oh, absolutely splendid!' Sebastian Holme spoke with a new animation. 'When he first began to take me around his bits of Africa and so on it was on the score of his needing a reliable lieutenant. That's how he represented it. But he really knew, I think.'

'Really knew? I don't follow you.'

'That it was what I needed if my painting was going to *be* painting, of course. Mind you, my painting was useful to *him*. If anybody got too curious about the yacht, I'd set up a whacking great canvas on the deck and start painting as showily as possible. I was a wealthy amateur, and Gregory was just the nautical character I hired to get me around exotic parts.'

'What was there about the yacht for people to get too curious about?'

'Well, of course, our main business was gun-running. You'd hardly believe the number of people in Africa that you can flog guns to. Guns are in. Just as gin and bibles are out.'

Braunkopf's catalogue, Cheel remembered, credited the Holme brothers with 'a small but highly significant import business'. This, presumably, was it.

'And other things as well?' he asked.

'We did a good deal with refugees. Choose any two territories with a seaboard, and you'll find quite a surprising two-way traffic of that sort.'

'And it was activities of that kind that got you into real trouble?'

'Lord, no.' Sebastian Holme seemed surprised. 'Gregory, you know, who stuck to these ploys, was never in serious trouble at all. It was quite *safe* being Gregory. That's why I turned into him.'

'You turned into him, I gather, after he was dead – which hardly suggests that his position was a safe one.'

'Oh, anybody can get killed in a riot, or in what they call a revolution. What Gregory was safe from was being nabbed by one or another government of the moment. Top blacks came and went, you know. They all had a notion that Gregory might be useful to them later on. My position was different. But how was I to know that the girl's wretched little husband was really Professor Ushirombo? There he was, peddling bicycles and bicycle tyres – they're dead keen on bicycles – in an obscure hamlet in the middle of the jungle. He was disguised and in hiding, you see. It wasn't a bit fair – was it?'

'They say all's fair in love and war – and I gather you were mixing up the two.' Cheel gave a cackle of laughter at this joke, but at once recovered himself. 'You're telling me,' he asked with distaste, 'that you were involved in some low *amour?*'

'Come off it, Cheel.'

'And this Professor Ushirombo, whose wife you seduced among the bicycle tyres – didn't he overthrow somebody?'

'The Professor overthrew the chap who called himself the Field-Marshal. Mbulu, his name was. He wasn't much of a one for the arts, or not what we think of as the arts over here. That was why my shirt was on Ushirombo, although I'd never set eyes on him. I mean although I *thought* I'd never set eyes on him. Actually, I'd locked him up in his own thunderbox.'

'His own what?'

'Kind of jakes. And there I was in that damned so-called hotel, arranging an exhibition of my paintings in honour of the liberator, who was said to be dead nuts on culture. And, all the time,

60

he was the little chap I'd lassoed and shut up for the night in the company of his own and other's ordures. It was just too funny. And now there he is, virtually a dictator, and I suppose the girl – a fabulous girl – is ensconced in the presidential palace, and calling herself the First Lady of Wamba.' Holme stared at Cheel. 'What are you making a face like that for?'

'I'm sorry.' Cheel realized that his indefatigable moral and aesthetic fastidiousness had betrayed him. He had no wish unnecessarily to offend Holme. 'I suppose I find something a little stiff in an affair with a female Hottentot.'

'Female Hottentot my foot. She was Eurasian and astounding. But all that's neither here nor there. It belongs to the past, worse luck.'

'I suppose the account given in Braunkopf's catalogue of the Wamba revolution and so on is quite inaccurate?'

'Sure to be, I'd say. As a matter of fact, I didn't read it. There were bits of poetry and God knows what. It looked revolting.'

'So it is. But go on, please, with your authentic narrative.'

'I don't see that there's much more that it's essential for you to know. I'm not hired to do you bedtime stories.' Holme looked sulky again as he made this childish remark. 'Of course there was the beard. That's rather crucial. You see, I'd been up country on my own just before this happened, and I hadn't bothered to shave. It's a thing I'd never done before – and I had realized that it made me look uncommonly like Gregory. And there was Gregory dead, you see, and all hell let loose outside – and by that time I knew that Ushirombo was out for my blood. Being cuckolded is a fearful insult among the Wamba. They simply don't live and let live. I'd have been boiled in oil – if I was lucky.'

'Is this Ushirombo a real professor?'

'Oh, yes – or at least he's a Ph. D. London, which must be the same thing. Civilized tastes. Collects pictures. But then so did Goering.'

'I'd suppose he'd have it in for your brother too – just because he *was* your brother. If he's as vengeful as you say, that is.'

'Oh, not at all. All his people had orders to treat Gregory very

61

respectfully. So had Mbulu's people, for that matter, and
Mkaka's people as well. It was as I told you: Gregory was much
too useful for any of the native parties to want to get across him.
He could whistle up guns for you almost as soon as you asked for
them.'

'Then there was no need for him – or you – to cut a way out
of the mob with a *prog*?'

'A *prog*? I never heard of it.'

'Or to board a *krimp*?'

'That's a Wamba word for a kind of yam sandwich.'

'It doesn't seem to me that there's an atom of truth in the
Da Vinci catalogue. It says that while your blessed hotel was
burning, Ushirombo and his lot were shut up in an old colonial
gaol.'

'Wherever he was, he was going to come out on top – whether
in hours or days. And there was poor old Gregory, beastly
dead.'

'You changed clothes with him?'

'Yes.'

'And cut off his beard and shaved him?'

'Yes. Of course it was rather bloody awful. But you shave a
corpse anyway, I'm told, if it's to go reasonably tidy to the grave.
And Gregory wouldn't have minded. He was a really decent
chap.'

'You left one of your sketch-books in his pocket?'

'Yes. I felt, you know, the job was worth doing well. But now
I rather wish I hadn't. It had some good things in it. Including a
few last-moment sketches of the actual attack on the hotel.'

'*That* was clever.' Cheel, although Holme's whole account
made him feel rather queasy, found himself unable to withhold
this tribute. 'But about the pictures. You're sure they all went
west?'

'Quite sure. I can't think why Hedda should suppose otherwise.
Except that she's an absolutely awful woman. Did I tell you that?
Mind you, *en déhanchement* – and specially with the weight on
the left leg – there's a particular tilt to her pelvis that would have

62

staggered Ingres. But there's nothing else to be said for her whatever.' Holme paused as if to consider for a moment. 'Or almost nothing,' he emended soberly.

'Did she ever make any of those African trips with Gregory and yourself?'

'Good Lord, no. Her only notion of travel is trips to Paris and trips back to New York.'

'Holme, you're *sure* one or two of those pictures of yours from the Wamba Palace mightn't turn up?'

'Quite sure.' Holme appeared puzzled by Cheel's compulsive return to this theme. 'You should have seen the place.'

'Your wife says she has a catalogue. Is that possible?'

'I suppose so. There was a catalogue. It was to be quite an affair, you see. Until Ushirombo turned out to be the little bicycle man, and until his taking over the government provoked all that chaos.'

'Did the catalogue state the dimensions of the pictures?'

'Yes, it did. It always gives a catalogue tone if you do that.'

'You've got a copy yourself?'

'Yes, I have – although I can't bear to look at it. You remember the chap in Shakespeare's play – not Macbeth but Mac-somebody-else? "All my pretty ones", he says. It's a real feeling.'

'Macduff's children were what you call beastly dead, and there was nothing to be done about it. But paintings can be – ' Cheel checked himself. 'What sort of people had seen them already: that whole set of canvases you'd done out there? Any other painters? Any critics, or fellows in the trade?'

'Of course not. There's nobody of that kind in those parts.'

'But some of them must have been viewed by people with some notion of painting? Cultivated amateurs, I mean. After all, they were *going* to be shown to some sort of public, as well as to the gratified Professor Ushirombo.'

'Yes, of course. But there was nobody who'd really have looked at them – except, of course, Gregory. The pinko-greys out there aren't exactly aesthetes, you know. They're business people who can't afford to be in business anywhere else. That and a handful

63

of ex-nigger-kicking police-officers on the way out. But I can't
see what you're getting at with all this.'

'Can't you, my dear chap?' This obtuseness on Sebastian
Holme's part positively put Cheel in a good humour. 'Well,
listen –'

Cheel broke off – aware that they were both suddenly listening
to something else. There had been a firm tread in the corridor
outside his undistinguished apartment. Now there was a thunder-
ous knock on the door.

11

'Oh, I say!' The noise had brought Sebastian Holme to his feet in
near-panic. 'Do you think that may be Hedda?'

'Most improbable – no need to be alarmed.' Cheel's tone belied
his assurance. The interruption, he was conjecturing to himself,
was by a person who had lately been making progressively insolent applications for the payment of rent. He moved towards the
door. 'If I just shoot that bolt, and if we keep quiet –'

It was too late. For the door had been thrown open with some
violence and a formidable presence had entered the room. The
man appeared, it was true, elderly or even old. But he stood well
over six feet, had a breadth of shoulder emphasized by a flowing
grey cloak worn with considerable *panache*, sported a broad-
brimmed black hat over a generous mane of silver hair, and was
carrying a long cane lightly flexed between two powerful hands.
He certainly wasn't going to be interested in the rent. Cheel didn't
at all like the look of him, all the same.

The stranger took a quick glance at the room's two occupants,
and then strode up to Holme.

'I wonder, now,' he said, 'if this would be the ruffian? Would
this, I ask myself, be the unspeakable blackguard I seek?' He
paused for a moment in this self-communion and stared fixedly
at Holme – the cane behaving in a rather ugly way in his grasp

64

meanwhile. 'I judge not. Yet isn't this fellow familiar to me?' He took one hand from the cane, and with the other flicked it in the air – and sufficiently sharply to make it produce a distinctly unpleasant hiss. He placed the free hand lightly on Holme's shoulder – an inoffensive, even if over-familiar, gesture which nevertheless made the young man jump as if upon the transmission of an electric current. 'I think I know you, don't I?' the stranger continued – making use, for the first time, of direct address.

'I don't think so. In fact, certainly not.' That Holme was almost totally unnerved was a fact evident to Cheel even through his own mounting alarm.

'You surprise me. In fact you fail to convince me.' The stranger stared at Holme harder still. 'Aren't you – ' He broke off. 'What's your name?' he asked. His voice as well as his stance was now minatory to an alarming pitch.

'My name?' For a moment Holme seemed totally helpless. 'I'm Sebas –' He managed to silence himself. 'My name's P-p-p–' It looked as if Holme, in a spurt of feeble invention, was trying to think of 'Pierce', 'Patterson', 'Pool' or some other plausible cognomen beginning with the arbitrarily chosen consonant. 'My name's P-p-p-icasso,' was what Holme managed to say.

'Most curious.' The stranger stood back a little. He might have been proposing to give himself elbow-room or arm-room. 'Do you know, that vaguely suggests itself to me as rather a Spanish-sounding name? Yet you don't look Spanish – not in the slightest degree.'

'A grandmother,' Holme said. 'I mean a grandfather, I had one Spanish grandfather. But the strain has rather bred itself out. You see I have quite a lot of Danish blood too.'

'Interesting,' the stranger said. 'But whether Spanish or Danish, I judge you not to be my man.' He swung round on Cheel. 'So now,' he said, 'I'd better take a look at *you*.'

Cheel backed away. Though intimidated, it wasn't escaping him that Sebastian Holme, despite his history of romantic places, had been intimidated too. Meanwhile, however, he himself was very intimidated indeed. For the stranger, tucking his cane under his arm, had produced from a pocket of his capacious cloak a newspaper which he now proceeded to unfold and to thrust under Cheel's nose.

'Perhaps,' the stranger said, 'you are familiar with the appearance of this?'

'Certainly not. I've never set eyes on it before.' It was – as always – with regret that Cheel had thus to commit himself to prevarication. But the exigency seemed to require it. Were Holme to join with him, indeed, in an instantaneous assault upon the intruder it was no doubt possible that they could, without too much damage to themselves, bundle him from the apartment. But Holme showed no sign of being available for any enterprise of the sort. He had simply sat down and was looking glum. 'It appears to be a newspaper,' Cheel said. 'A provincial newspaper. Let me see.' He affected to peer more closely at the outspread page. 'Circulating in some God-forsaken industrial hole in the Midlands.'

'The God-forsaken industrial hole,' the stranger said, 'happens to be the town in which I was born and grew up. Although no longer frequently resident, I am in the enjoyment, I am proud to say, of good repute among my former fellow-citizens. There are those who have been kind enough to say that I am a credit to them.'

'I'm delighted to hear it,' Cheel said. 'Of course I don't know why they should cherish such a notion – but I'm delighted to hear it all the same.' He took a further couple of steps backwards as he spoke. This utterly irrational person – it had occurred to him – might be prompted to treat a delicate witticism as a stroke of insolence.

'Um.' For the moment, the stranger did no more than eye Cheel appraisingly. 'May I ask if you are familiar with the name of Albert Rumbelow?'

'Rumbelow?' Cheel looked thoughtful. '*Albert* Rumbelow? I believe I am. I think – Yes, he was surely a painter. Didn't he go in for vast daubs depicting coronations and civic centres and new bridges and anything else that was large enough? He must have

66

been enormously hard-working, as well as totally untalented. Dead now, probably. Cheel would know.'

'Cheel?' the stranger repeated ominously.

'Mervyn Cheel. Fellow who lives in this flat. Merely in a temporary way, I believe. I was hoping to find him in. Decided to wait for him.'

'I see.' There could be little doubt that the stranger did entirely see. 'I am Albert Rumbelow – as you may guess.'

'How do you do,' Cheel said. 'This is –' With his usual high regard for formal manners, he had been about to pronounce some introductory words on Holme. It seemed absurd, however, to say 'This is Mr Pablo Picasso.' 'This,' he emended, 'is another friend of Mr Cheel's.'

'Indeed. I am surprised. I am surprised that a creature so base and venomous as this Cheel should have friends. Or enemies, for that matter. For who would break a butterfly' – he gave a whisk in the air with his cane – 'let alone a valuable weapon upon a Cheel?'

'I am afraid I fail to understand you.' Mr Albert Rumbelow's absurd perversion of the poet Pope had, very naturally, further offended Cheel. 'If you have any message that you would care to leave –'

'I am inclined to think that you are not yourself the man Cheel.'

'Precisely,' Cheel interrupted, much relieved.

'It is true that you make an unfavourable impression on me. I should judge you to be petty, dishonest and malign. It seems likely, however, that this Cheel is even more loathsome.'

'Exactly,' Cheel said emphatically.

'It would be my conjecture that his outward appearance answers pretty clearly to the inward man. In which case he can hardly be distinguishable from a toad. I would wish him to know that this is the expectation in which I came to see him.'

'Certainly,' Cheel said, and edged hopefully towards the door. 'I'll tell him exactly what you've said.'

'But there is rather more. I am at present engaged in executing a series of very large wall-paintings on canvas. The theme running through them is the British Way of Life, and they are intended to embellish what is to be called, I understand, a Palace of Industry in one of the new Commonwealth countries. Several have been exhibited, and I have already given much thought to the design of several more. Sketches for these are to be seen in the present Exhibition of the Royal Academy.'

'I'm delighted to hear it,' Cheel said.

'The earlier examples were favourably, or at least candidly, received by numerous critics. Some made adverse comments of a rational kind which I hope have been helpful to me. And your friend Mr Cheel wrote in *this*.' Once more, the abominable Rumbelow held up the newspaper. 'It is a respectable journal – but not in a position, I imagine, to retain the service of an art critic of any standing in London. What Cheel – who is so clearly of no account – has to say would be of no moment to me but for one circumstance: that he has sought to ridicule me in the eyes of persons among whom I happen to have grown up. You follow me?'

'Oh, quite,' Cheel said. 'Oh, perfectly. I'll put all this to Cheel.'

'Cheel did not, indeed, as you have kindly done, suggest that I am dead. His preferred word is "moribund". And works to which I have given many years of honest application – and to which, although of advanced age, I must of necessity give as many more as are granted to me – your friend describes as dotages unredeemed even by the genuine pathos of waning powers. What he has printed, in fact, is not criticism but insult.'

'Dear me,' Cheel said. 'Quite shocking. I shall suggest a letter of apology. Would you like me to call a taxi?'

'I should not accept an apology. I consider an apology valid only when it passes between gentlemen.'

'Quite so. I see your point.' Cheel had managed to reach the door. He was now courteously holding it open. 'You might consider a libel action, I suppose. Although such things are always tricky – and expensive.'

'As it happens, I am not a litigant. I am a duellist.'

'I beg your pardon?' Cheel had jumped at these incredible words.

'I remarked, sir, that I am not a litigant but a duellist. I would have the person Cheel informed that, should he to my knowledge offer me the shadow of a further impertinence on the occasion of the exhibition of my new designs, I will call him to account. Should he decline such a challenge' – and Rumbelow tossed the newspaper on the floor and gave a flourish with his cane – 'he may expect a thrashing. Be so good as to tell him so.' Rumbelow strode to the door. Then he paused, turned round, and took another long look at Holme. 'As for this young man,' he said, 'I am disposed to wish him better company. He seems familiar to me, as I said. I hope he is not quite so foolish as the few remarks he has offered would appear to suggest. Good afternoon to you both.'

The door banged. The outrageous old person was gone.

12

'That was a pretty narrow shave, wasn't it?' Sebastian Holme said, as Rumbelow's footsteps mercifully faded.

'I should have been sorry if he had ventured upon violence. He's an elderly man, and restraining him would have been painful.' Cheel spoke with dignity. 'But I can't say I feel I've escaped something.'

'Oh, you!' Holme offered this with an indignant snort. 'I was thinking of myself. There was a point at which it almost looked as if the chap was going to recognize me.'

'Did you recognize *him*? Are you conscious of ever having seen him before?'

'Well, yes – I rather feel I am. I couldn't have put a name to him, but I do have a notion we may have met.'

'You're sure he *didn't* recognize you?'

'How can I tell?' Holme was impatient. 'Even if he didn't, he may suddenly remember later on. In that case, there will be the devil to pay. I'll have to run for it again – if I don't want Ushirombo to get me.'

'I'm not very clear about just that.' Cheel sat down on a contraption that turned at night into a not very satisfactory bed. He felt extremely tired. All day he appeared to have been battling with irrational, violent and disagreeable people. If nothing were to come of all this harassment, he would feel very ill-used indeed. 'Ushirombo and his revolution are thousands of miles away. How can he really get you, now that you've shown him a clean pair of heels?'

'Extradition.'

'But surely they wouldn't extradite you for pinching his girl for a night? I gathered that was about the size of it.'

'You don't understand. He'd say it was something quite different and absolutely criminal. And he'd be sure to get his way with those rotten chaps in Whitehall. Ushirombo has been recognized, you see, and they're sucking up to him like mad. Wamba is still in the Commonwealth, you know. Ushirombo will be coming to Prime Ministers' Conferences, and so on. There's no standing up against that.'

'I suppose not.' Cheel was not dissatisfied with this further elucidation. The more scared Holme was the better. 'So, as far as that fellow Rumbelow is concerned, we must just hope for the best. By the way, what he was saying, needless to say, was mere offensive nonsense.'

'You mean you didn't write those things about him in that paper?'

'Oh, yes – I wrote them, all right.' Cheel gave his cackle of laughter. 'You see, Rumbelow's been almost totally a failure. He has no talent whatever.'

'I'd have thought that to be a reason for leaving him alone, rather. I'd suppose you'd keep really rude remarks for somebody who had plenty of talent and was perversely abusing it.'

'I think we'd better be getting back to business.' Cheel saw no occasion for wasting time on pitiful notions like this. It was mysterious that so stupid a person as Sebastian Holme appeared to be should have the ability to paint like an angel – if angels did paint, in their off-moments from blowing trumpets and singing

70

hymns. Holme's talent, in fact, was just one more instance of the general injustice of things. However, Cheel was determined that, for once, there should be a bit of fair play. 'And our business,' he went on, 'is to get you painting again. You feel you can't, so to speak, begin from dot?'

'Of course I can't. I'm *me*. Surely that's clear. I can only go on from where I left off. And, in present circumstances, I could only do *that*, you see, more or less for my own private amusement. Which *ought* to be all right, I suppose. Only it isn't. It may be shameful, but I need acknowledgement and a public.'

'Open and direct acknowledgement?'

'Well, what I create, I have to give to the world. Something like that. And give as Sebastian Holme.'

'You wouldn't be content simply to go on painting Holmes, and stacking them against the wall?'

'No, I wouldn't. And anyway, I haven't got a wall – or quite soon I shan't have one. So that's no good.'

'I see.' To Cheel's mind, the discussion was now developing very well. 'But must it be Holme? Why not take a new name, and carry on under it from just where you are?'

'Rubbish!' Holme gave his impatient snort. 'Everybody would say that some unknown bloody man had turned up and was doing miserable, incompetent *pastiches* of the late Sebastian Holme. You yourself, for instance, Cheel. I can just see you making your nasty sort of jeering fun at the untalented mug's expense.'

'*I* can see all that.' Cheel's agreement was cheerful and immediate. 'Now, let's put it this way. You could do with quite a lot of money?'

'Of course I could. Gregory's is running out, as I told you. And one needs the beastly stuff all the time.'

'And when you die you want to leave more Sebastian Holmes behind you?'

'Just that. It's lunacy, I suppose. But just that.'

'There's nothing simpler – nothing simpler than combining these *two* aims.' Cheel cackled as Holme stared at him. 'Only you

71

won't, in the main, be able, as you put it, to go on from where you are. You'll have to step back a bit. Is my meaning clear?'

'I don't know what you're talking about.'

'Well, well!' Cheel laughed tolerantly before this obtuseness. 'You must paint those lost pictures over again. We've got a catalogue. We've got the dimensions. You must remember pretty well what they were like. Once they exist again – don't you see? – their provenance will be unchallengeable.'

'You're crazy, Cheel. They were destroyed –'

'And a good thing, too. It wouldn't do if they began to turn up after you'd painted them all over again. '

Holme got up and walked about the room. He seemed to be back in one of his phases of bewilderment.

'You claim to be damned smart, and then you talk nonsense. Everybody *knows* they were destroyed.'

'It's that that's nonsense, my dear chap. *You* know they were destroyed – or think you do. Braunkopf's stupid catalogue says they were destroyed. But not everybody. Your wife doesn't, for instance.'

'That's just part of Hedda's being so awful.'

'Well, it's useful, all the same. And as she appears to believe that almost anybody she sets eyes on is in some conspiracy about the things, her persuasion is bound to spread. The rumour that perhaps some of the paintings weren't destroyed – even that none of them was destroyed – will go round. Quietly, I hope. We don't want any crude publicity. Just a whispered word on what people are saying will be precisely right when I start unloading your re-created masterpieces on eager collectors. The Wamba catalogue, with its titles and precise dimensions, will serve to authenticate the pictures, as I said. After that, the deals will be on the basis of No Questions Asked.'

'But Hedda would be sure to hear of what's going on. And she'd claim the lot.'

'She wouldn't have a hope. Not the way I'd fix it.' Cheel radiated modest confidence. 'You'll see.'

'I don't want to see.' Holme, still prowling, gave a sulky kick at Cheel's waste-paper basket. 'I don't want to produce replicas of old stuff. That's not what I call painting, at all.'

'That's not the way to think of it.' Cheel maintained his tolerant and kindly note – although inwardly he was wondering whether he had already come to the moment at which it would be appropriate to turn on the heat. 'You can give yourself, my dear chap, to the absorbing task of improving on every one of them. Even to improving the composition, within bounds, since it seems unlikely that the new paintings will ever be seen by anybody who has an informed memory of the old ones.'

'I suppose that's true.' Holme scowled irresolutely. 'I can see myself doing that – for a time. But there's no future in it.'

'That's what you say about your present position – and quite rightly. But just paint those pictures again, and things will be different. It's a matter of money, in the first place. Make some money – and, actually, you can make a small fortune – and you will be able to clear out to where you please. There must be some perfectly agreeable countries that don't have extradition treaties, or whatever they're called, with this vindictive chap Ushirombo. Or Ushirombo may be turfed out of Wamba.'

'That's true.' For the first time, Holme brightened. 'One day I suppose he may.'

'Meantime, what we want is quite a little money – just to fix you up and get you going. I suppose I could look around for some. But probably what's left in Gregory's account will serve. To rent a studio, and so on.'

'A studio?' Having taken a further and more cheerful kick at the waste-paper basket, Holme glanced around him. 'This place will do very well. It's got a decent light, as I said.'

'This place? Well, that would be fine.' Cheel was careful to keep any note of rash triumph out of his voice. 'Only it's rather cramped quarters for two, wouldn't you say?'

'Not for two. For one.' Holme gave his sudden grin. 'You clear out, Cheel. You've got your own permanent place somewhere else – or so you said. You can get back there when the decorating's finished.'

'All that is rather indefinite.' Cheel spoke with dignity. 'It will be better –'

'Does anybody ever come around this place – a woman to clean, or anything like that?' Holme kicked a puff of dust out of the carpet. 'I shouldn't suppose so.'

'My needs are very simple.' Cheel maintained the dignified note. 'Nobody comes here – except an occasional man about the electricity.' He considered. 'And the rent,' he added.

'They wouldn't be interested in whether it's one or another face that greets them at the door?'

'Probably not, if there's a spot in cash to hand over.'

'Good. You walk out, Cheel, and I walk in.' Holme was displaying an unexpected power of rapid decision. 'My needs are pretty simple too. For the moment' – he glanced consideringly at Cheel – 'they don't go beyond a clean pair of sheets. But for the moment, too, you can do the coming and going. You can bring in the drink and the provisions, I mean, and also the necessary stuff from the colourman. Presumably you know enough to make a more or less intelligent job of that.'

'It's conceivable,' Cheel said with irony. 'But I think you'd better do that yourself, all the same.'

'Not if you're hankering after an early start, Cheel. I don't stir from this room till I've grown that beard again.'

'Very well. And that settles it.'

'Not quite, Cheel. I paint the things. You market them. We've got to settle our terms.'

'Oh, that!' Cheel made an easy gesture. 'The project's on velvet, my dear chap. So we're not likely to quarrel there.'

'We'd better not.' Holme gave Cheel a hard look.

'We'd better not,' Cheel said, and gave Holme a hard look back.

Part Two

13

Cheel drew up by the kerb – neatly, considering that it was some time since he had driven a car. For more months than he cared to remember, indeed, he had been constrained to the indignity of travel by public conveyance, and it was satisfactory to return, in this small particular, to his proper social level. The beauty of simply hiring a car was that, on a short term view, you could afford to hire a rather grand one. The bill for this one would become oppressive, say, over a six months' period. But by that time his circumstances, which had so notably improved over the past few weeks, would have improved very much further again. Meanwhile, he attributed his early successes in his present enterprise to driving up to significant appointments in a sober Rolls-Royce.

And from a Rolls, too, one only had to raise a beckoning finger to have the paper-seller scurrying across the pavement. The fellow wasn't going to get out of one a halfpenny more than he would get out of the shabbiest pedestrian in the street. He tumbled over himself, nevertheless. Cheel, observing this phenomenon now, regarded it with a double satisfaction. It was alike a just tribute to his own importance and an index of the thoroughly sound state of English society. It was possible, of course, that in the dim minds of those paper-vending persons there harboured atavistic memories of toffs, swells and gov'nors who tossed you a crown or a half-sovereign while you splashed happily in the mud from their hansom cab. Nobody could scatter that sort of largess nowadays; the grim fact of penal taxation forbade it. Nevertheless the hearts of newspaper boys still beat in the right place.

Cheel completed his transaction with a threepenny bit. What

had prompted this expenditure was a scrawled poster that had caught his eye as he drove. It read:

USHIROMBO
FOR
LONDON

Cheel scanned the front page. Yes, the news from Wamba was given some prominence. The Secretary of State for Commonwealth Relations had invited Professor Ushirombo to pay a visit and he would almost certainly do so. The political stability of Wamba was now such that its Prime Minister could leave the government of the country with perfect confidence to his senior ministers. Informed circles in Wamba-Wamba inclined to the view that JUMBO – the terrorist organization of the fanatical 'Emperor' Mkaka – had virtually disintegrated. The standard of living was advancing rapidly. During his stay in London Professor Ushirombo would meet leading industrialists and discuss with them various plans for economic development. But it was also known that – as might be expected of one with his background in education – he was particularly anxious to arrange for cultural exchanges. The Wamba Male Choir was definitely coming to Britain. It was not impossible that the Wamba State Ballet might come as well.

Cheel read this with satisfaction. He was all for Ushirombo settling in as chief boss of the Wamba for keeps. But the paper, it seemed, had more to say. The column ended with:

Wamba-Wamba Diary. See p. 6.

Glancing at his watch, Cheel made to drive on. Then he remembered that he was now among those by whom others expect to be kept waiting. So he turned to p. 6. That was another thing about sitting in a car like this. The police jolly well knew to what class (or perhaps it should be called income-group) one belonged. There was no unmannerly intrusion of helmeted heads or talk about No Waiting. Here again England showed itself to be as sound as a bell.

Wamba-Wamba Diary ran to a couple of columns. The diarist was Our African Correspondent. He seemed to like the place very much. A sub-editor had emphasized its general jollity with appropriate captions. There was *Wamba Women Go Gay*, which was about a pilgrim from Detroit opening a Strip-Tease Club. There was *Urgent Penal Reform*, from which it appeared that Professor Ushirombo was building a large new prison. There was *Top Raphael for Wamba World Fair?* – announcing that the Professor had some thought of borrowing the Madonna di Foligno from the Pope. And there was *Nijinsky Eclipsed*, a stiffly statistical bit about just how high the male dancers of the Wamba State Ballet could leap vertically in the air – and this while continuing to wave their clubs and spears vigorously above their heads. Finally there was a paragraph about an Englishman called Wutherspoon who, although formerly a pillar of the old colonial order, had become a close personal friend of Professor Ushirombo. Wutherspoon, who had lately left Wamba for England and well-earned retirement, might be expected to be a mine of information about the new Member of the Commonwealth.

Cheel finished Wamba-Wamba Diary in a spirit of tolerant amusement. It was all to the good that the outlandish place should thus be going on the map, since it would give collectors (the most moronic of mortals) a muzzy sense that, in investing in a chunk of Wamba jungle as painted by Sebastian Holme, they were at the same time in on the ground floor of an expanding economy. The corpulent man, for instance – to whom he had owed what champagne he got at the Holme Exhibition – the corpulent man had a mind that would move in precisely that way.

But more corpulent men were needed. Cheel stuffed away his newspaper and – before letting his car glide imperceptibly into rapid motion – soberly considered this problem. His present mission was tied up with it.

The governing fact, of course, was that things had been going remarkably well. Sebastian Holme was indeed painting like an angel – and, for that matter, like a demon into the bargain. There was something uncanny about the manner in which, in a dingy North London attic, he could conjure up before his inward eye the minute particularities of an exotic landscape, or the precise complementaries lurking in the shadow cast by some ebony savage. And the job had absorbed him from the first, and was continuing to absorb him. Contrary to Cheel's expectations, Holme had been simply no trouble at all. It was true that he had at first considerably inconvenienced his discoverer by insisting on appropriating his living-quarters as he had. But now, of course, Cheel was able to do considerably better for himself. This was something that Holme might quite reasonably have felt as applying to himself too. Yet nothing of the sort had happened. The odd chap seemed perfectly content with the shabby attic. Indeed – so far as Cheel's knowledge went – he hadn't once ventured out of it. Although he had grown his beard again, he hadn't again in any effective way become Gregory Holme, except in the matter of having written out and handed to Cheel a single cheque representing the balance of what had lain in Gregory's account.

This was all beautifully as it should be. Initially, indeed, Cheel had viewed it with some alarm. Holme (although, when visited, occasionally sulky or rude) gave the effect of having disappeared as a person altogether. What inhabited Cheel's former domain was no more than a preternaturally sensitive machine for turning stretches of canvas and tubes of paint into glowing evocations of things Cheel himself had never set eyes on. It was a set-up that appeared a little too good to be true, and at first Cheel had been apprehensively on his guard against the irruption, through this dedicated artist, of what might be called the diurnal man – the man, for instance, who had married Hedda, and who had enjoyed the favours of Professor Ushirombo's lady after having locked up the Professor himself in a place of peculiar indignity. But for weeks there had been no sign of anything of the sort. Cheel's anxieties had therefore abated. It looked as if money from Holme *was* just that.

It was the painter's blameless industry, indeed, that was

creating a problem for Cheel now. Holme's first two re-creatings of Wamba pictures – 'Mourning Dance with Torches' and 'Fishing Cats at Pool' – had been achieved with astonishing speed. And Cheel had managed to sell them equally promptly: hence his present prosperity. It was clear that the Wamba catalogue, together with a colourful story about how just two or three of the pictures listed in it had been saved, would provide a perfectly respectable provenance for more than a score of further efforts on Holme's part. And moreover – provided the things were unloaded quietly enough as they became available – there was no reason why the sort of prices that had been obtained by Braunkopf should not be maintained and even surpassed.

There was, however, a real problem. Cheel's direct access either to individuals or to institutions likely to pay the right price for a Sebastian Holme was somewhat restricted – surprisingly so, he reflected, in the light of his acknowledged eminence as a critic. It was undeniable that the unfortunate misunderstanding over the Nicolaes de Staël still hung about the fringes of people's minds. This was awkward in itself. So was the fact that he could point to no genuine connexion with Holme during what the world thought of as Holme's lifetime. Although it was credible, therefore, that one or two of Holme's supposedly destroyed pictures should have come his way, suspicion would almost certainly be aroused if it became known that he appeared to enjoy a corner in the things. Some years before, and purely as a matter of disinterested intellectual pursuit, he had made a rather careful study of the conditions and mechanics of the forger's craft in the sphere of painting. It had been his conclusion that much the most tricky part of the business was the choosing of the channel or channels by which the products were fed into the market. Anything like a bottle-neck was dangerous; except in certain very special circumstances, the things should bear the appearance of coming from here, there and everywhere.

But there *was* something of a special circumstance in this case. A single dealer had lately exhibited and marketed almost the entire *œuvre* of Sebastian Holme as it was known to exist. And these were all unchallengeable. If further pictures began quietly to appear, far the best person to find unquestioning purchasers for them would be the proprietor of the Da Vinci Gallery. That was why Cheel – thus impressively turned out in his very grand car – was on his way to see Hildebert Braunkopf now.

There were risks: Braunkopf's association with Hedda Holme was one of these – and it was difficult to tell whether it was increased or lessened by the fact that Hedda so plainly didn't trust him. There was a possible financial disadvantageousness; Braunkopf was avaricious (a trait Cheel detested) and might try to strike the same outrageous sort of bargain that he had struck with the artist's supposed widow. There were also some uncomfortably large imponderables; for example, Cheel wasn't quite sure just what degree of dishonesty (to put the matter with impossible crudeness) Braunkopf would regard as all in the day's work. But of course he wasn't going to trust Braunkopf with the truth – or not until he was very sure of his ground.

All in all, Mervyn Cheel felt very pleasantly on top of things. Gliding smoothly down Piccadilly, he took leisure to consider the amenities around him, and to plan the rest of the day for himself once Braunkopf had been disposed of. He might drive on to Savile Row, and amuse himself by charitably renewing relations with a tailor who had behaved rather tiresomely about a bill some years before. Then there was Burlington House; one could park with considerable *éclat* in the courtyard there, and while away an hour amid the absurdities on view at the Royal Academy's Summer Exhibition. The outrageous Rumbelow, he remembered, had more of his dotages on display. He owed Rumbelow something. Perhaps an inspection of his latest rubbish might prompt him to a fresh witticism or two which could be given currency as soon as the Holme enterprise had become so lucrative as to afford Cheel a safe and agreeable retreat on the continent. But that was for the future. At the moment, he need consider no more than a pleasant conclusion to what was going to prove, he felt, a thoroughly propitious day. He was now cruising past Green Park Station. The Ritz was on his right and the

Berkeley on his left. His tastes, he reflected, although refined, were very simple, after all. At one or other of these modest places he could pick up a very tolerable evening meal.

14

As the Rolls drew up before the Da Vinci Gallery the door of that establishment opened, and its proprietor appeared, beaming. It was evident that some system obtained whereby he was instantly apprised of the advent of anything so promising. Braunkopf paused, however, in somewhat unflattering surprise when he became aware of the car's occupant.

'Ah,' he exclaimed, 'the goot –' He checked himself. 'Ah,' he amended, 'my dear Mr Cheel!' He held out his pudgy hand. 'Vot privileges, yes?' He was peering into the interior of the vehicle. 'There is a lady, no?'

'A lady?' Descending to the pavement, Cheel repeated this in surprise. 'Certainly there isn't a lady.'

'No lady.' Braunkopf seemed disappointed. 'Sometimes, when there is sudden affluences, a lady is the explosion.' He looked appraisingly at Cheel. 'But, no, you have not the physicals for what I have in brain, yes? So there is some other explosion. Perhaps you have won on the Ponds.'

Cheel was wholly displeased by these remarks. It was mortifying to be considered in the light of a failed gigolo, and even more mortifying to be credited with the plebeian practice of filling up football coupons. He refrained, however, from comment, and took a quick look at the exterior of the Da Vinci instead. Its window had been relined with a richly sombre and indubitably ancient brocade. There was now a fine steel mesh against the inner surface of the glass. And this was a reasonable precaution. The only object visible in the window was a figure in greenish wax, about six inches high. Cheel had no difficulty in identifying it. The piece of sculpture for which it was a maquette

83

was to be found perched above the tomb of the Duke of Nemours in the New Sacristy of San Lorenzo in Florence.

'Is that really by Michelangelo?' Cheel asked – and noted with satisfaction that he had managed to say something insulting to Braunkopf in his turn.

'Most puttikler authentink *chef-d'œuvre* of Buonarroti straight from Firenze, Mr Cheel.'

'Straight from Florence? Well, well! Perhaps you picked it up in a little shop on the *Ponte Vecchio*?'

'The piece has been purchased by a representation of the Da Vinci Gallery.' Braunkopf spoke with dignity. 'Our special representation in Firenze made this purchasings private collection a nobleman resident in the city.'

'I know some of these people, naturally. What's your nobleman's name?'

'Medici,' Braunkopf said firmly. 'The Marchese Lorenzo di Medici. Or possibilities the Conte Cosimo di Medici. No doubtings, Mr Cheel, you know them both.'

'Most interesting.' Cheel flattered himself that he turned an urbane face to this impertinent nonsense. 'And now, I think, I'll come inside. I've something to talk about.'

'Vot privileges!' Braunkopf murmured once more. Although he was not on this occasion sporting a gardenia, his attire – Cheel noticed – still struck an Edwardian note of sober richness and vulgarity nicely blended. 'Vot a happiness!' Braunkopf added for good measure, and led the way inside.

The Da Vinci itself was transformed. The plushy settees had been re-plushed, and were now keeping company with a number of French pieces which Cheel at a glance admitted to be genuine. There were pictures only sparely on the walls, and none of them was modern. The only modern picture in evidence, indeed, was an early Braque, and this appeared to be in rather careless use as a fire-screen. All the others were Italian, and few of their painters seemed to have lived beyond the threshold of the *quattrocento*. 'Buonamico di Cristofano, *detto* Buffalmacco,' Cheel read on the first label. 'Giovanni da Santo Stefano a Ponte.' 'Gherardo di Jacopo Starnina.' 'Parri di Spinello Spinelli.' A lot of the names seemed to be longer than the pictures they accompanied were broad, and the total effect was eminently decorous and impressively arcane. Braunkopf was now demonstrably after a stratum of collectors totally different from the people who buy things to impress each other with when hung in yachts tied up in Menton or Cannes. Probably – Cheel thought – not such quick money by a long way. In the long term, this more austere policy might pay off richly enough. Meanwhile, it seemed possible that Braunkopf was hazardously extending himself on the financial side. Which was very much all to the good.

Braunkopf led the way into his inner sanctum. It now contained nothing but a plain olive-wood table and two forbiddingly uncomfortable medieval chairs. The walls were bare. But in the middle of the room was a richly draped easel, on which stood a small picture, glowing under a discreet spotlight. Cheel walked up to it – principally because this seemed to be what Braunkopf expected him to do.

'Good Lord!' Cheel was really surprised. Here too was an early Italian work. But this time it was Venetian – and very delicious. St George's horse contrived to be at once chunky and improbably curvilinear; St George himself – who seemed to be about twelve – was spearing a dragon that looked like a lavishly bejewelled starfish; the lady – behind whom was the most exquisite little town – was making a gesture of mild deprecation and surprise. 'Montorfano?' Cheel asked. 'There's something like it in the Martinengo at Brescia.'

'Quirico da Murano, Mr Cheel.' Braunkopf made this correction with a lofty courtesy. 'Acquired from Cardinal Borgia. And this veek's authentink Braunkopf. Always on this easel – yes? – the authentink Braunkopf painting of the veek. And in the vindow, the authentink Braunkopf sculpture of the veek.'

'So the Michelangelo's an authentic Braunkopf too?'

'Puttikler so, Mr Cheel.' Braunkopf made a large gesture towards one of the bone-jarring chairs. 'Please take place,' he said amiably. 'A glass of dry Madeira, no?' He touched a muted bell.

Cheel allowed himself to be provided with the refreshment suggested. There were some small, dry biscuits too. It was all very remote from the Sebastian Holme Private View: the crush, the urgent youthful pictures, the champagne. A slight uneasiness (unworthy of a general initiating a bold strategic conception) beset Cheel. Braunkopf continued to be a ridiculous person – but it wasn't quite clear that Cheel had precisely taken the measure of him. Probably a direct attack would be best.

'What I've come in about,' Cheel said, 'is Sebastian Holme.'

'Holme? *Sebastian* Holme?' Braunkopf appeared to make a slight effort of memory. 'Ah, yes – but of course. A young man with so much of the promisings. So far as any of the moderns has promisings, no? You and I, my dear and goot Mr Cheel, have the understanding of the great classical traditions, yes? But Holme was goot. Yes, Holme was quite goot. And the little posthumous show here in the Da Vinci: that we can be arrogant of. We secured provisions for his wife in her aggrievement. Yes, we take the modest arrogance in that.'

'No doubt.' Cheel thought as poorly of these sentiments as he did of Braunkopf's command of his Sovereign's English. 'I suppose you've heard that more Holmes have been turning up?'

'More Holmes?' Braunkopf looked mildly surprised. 'More brothers? More aggrieved wives?'

'You know very well I mean nothing of the sort. More of Sebastian Holme's pictures. They weren't destroyed in that revolution, or riot, or whatever it was. I mean, not all of them were. The stuff you printed in your catalogue was all my eye and Betty Martin.'

'Betty Martin?' This homely locution was beyond Braunkopf. 'A mistress, yes?'

'I mean that you pretty well made it up – or got somebody else to make it up. I have my ear to the ground, you know. And I've heard that a couple of the Wamba pictures have turned up. And

86

there are others that *can* turn up. In fact I can probably lay my hands on them myself.'

'This is very great nonsenses, Mr Cheel.' Braunkopf made a careless gesture – but Cheel was encouraged to see that his eyes had a little narrowed in his puffy face. 'It is the English jokings, I think. Ha-ha-ha, yes?'

'You must know that his wife believes that the things survived? I'd be surprised to hear that she didn't accuse you of sitting on them.'

'Mrs Holme is an endeavouring person – a most puttikler endeavouring person. I was glad when our association termited.'

'I can well believe it. But, you know, you can be a little trying yourself. This game of treating Holme as something inconsiderable in a dim past. Come off it, Braunkopf.'

'Come off it?' Braunkopf, who had seated himself on the second of the impossible chairs, rose and peered at the hard wooden surface thus revealed. 'This is more jokings, yes? This is the japes, no?'

'There's no joking about it. Would you like to see No. 18?'

Braunkopf, who had sat down again, reached out and returned the stopper to the decanter of Madeira. He might have been indicating that no further refreshment would be provided in return for enigmatical talk of this character.

'You know,' Cheel went on, 'that there was a printed catalogue of that exhibition in the Wamba Palace Hotel? In fact, you've no doubt seen a copy?'

'Mrs Holme's.' Braunkopf nodded, perhaps a shade unwarily. 'Natchally, I had it copied for myself.'

'Very good. Have a look at No. 18, and you'll find it's called "Clouded Leopards Playing". And the dimensions are given in inches. $39\frac{3}{8}$ by $21\frac{1}{2}$. Slightly odd proportions – but Holme made a notable thing of them. And – as I say – the picture's now in my car.'

'*Your* car, Mr Cheel?' Braunkopf managed something of a come-back with this emphasis.

'My car.'

'In fack you already been selling one two more Holmes, yes?'

'Ah – that is confidentials, my goot Mr Braunkopf.'

This witticism – surprisingly ill-bred in a man of Cheel's polished manners – did not appear to disturb Braunkopf. Perhaps he was unaware of it. But at least he again took the stopper out of the decanter.

'If you could sell one two more Holmes,' he said almost musingly, 'you could sell three four. But you could not sell ten twenty. That why you come here.'

'Precisely.' Cheel spoke as a candid man boldly laying his cards on the table.

'It deserves the considerings.' Braunkopf made an acquiescent gesture. 'So bring in your leopards.'

With proper dignity, Cheel produced a key from his waistcoat pocket. 'It's on the back seat,' he said. 'One of your people can fetch it.'

15

'But of course,' Cheel said ten minutes later, 'you have to consider the possibility of its being a forgery.' He stepped back from 'Clouded Leopards Playing' as if a more synoptic view might assist his own mind to greater clarity on this point. 'Particularly as I'm not able, at this stage, to say very much more. To a certain extent, I must consider myself under instructions. There are principals in the affair.'

'The Da Vinci, Mr Cheel, always insists on the goot principles. It is a puttikler ethical concern.'

'I mean persons for whom I am acting. The whole operation, of course, would have to be kept as confidential as possible. That would be in your interest, acting as my agent. If it became known that a large number of further Holmes were coming on the market, prices would drop at once.'

'They will drop in any cases, Mr Cheel.' Braunkopf shook his head despondently. 'Holme was a vogue, yes? You must not have the expectings of high prices, if I handle this. Sales – perhaps. The big moneys – no.'

'That remains to be examined.' Cheel smiled indulgently at this primitive guile. 'But there is, you know, the prior question which I've just mentioned. The paintings' – he gestured towards the leopards – 'may be forgeries. And this one for a start. Consider.' He raised a hand as if to forestall some over-facile denial of this on Braunkopf's part. 'When an artist dies young, and his work is scarce and in great demand, there will always exist a strong motive –'

'Nonsenses!' Braunkopf, who had been peering into the canvas with a ferocious concentration uncharacteristic of him, pronounced this emphatically. 'It is by Holme. It is No. 18. It is the "Clouded Leopards Playing", without any doubtings at all.'

'Mightn't it be wise to have another opinion – confidentially, of course? There are one or two people who could make a fairly reliable expertise.'

'I make my own expertises, my goot Mr Cheel. And this is an authentink Sebastian Holme.'

'Very well. We have only to discuss terms, and it can become an authentic Braunkopf, as you like to say, as well.'

Braunkopf shook his head. He rose, walked over to the easel, and appeared sombrely to contemplate the authentic Braunkopf of the week. Quirico da Murano, he might have been reflecting, stood for a sort of higher reputability in the art-dealing world from which he would be reluctant to see the Da Vinci Gallery retreat upon the dubious courses proposed by this visitor. And Cheel once more felt misgivings. Was it possible, he wondered, that Braunkopf was as passing honest as Providence has made it possible for a picture dealer to be? What if the man were to pick up his telephone and call the police? Or what if he at once communicated to Hedda Holme the fact that her suspicions about the Wamba pictures appeared to have had substance after all? These were disturbing speculations. Cheel waited in some suspense.

'Mrs Holme,' Braunkopf said – so that Cheel jumped. 'We are to make no divulgings to her, no?'

'Definitely not.' Cheel spoke with emphasis – and with relief. The crucial corner, he felt, had been turned. Braunkopf was coming in.

'But she would hear of such dealings, no? Already she has those suspectings – and she has freunts, my goot Cheel, the great vorlt of art. Once twice we might keep a deal dark – but third fourth time the cat would be in the bag.' Braunkopf nodded impressively. 'The cat would be in the bag, and there would be a pretty kettle of hornets. You are suggesting the impossibles.'

'You think she would claim the pictures? It's conceivable, no doubt.' Cheel advanced this in a judicial manner. 'But she'd make no headway, you know. Possession is enormously important in such cases. The whole onus would be on her to make out a case. The pictures have been marketable commodities from the moment Holme finished painting them. And he was out there in Wamba and his wife was here in England. She just couldn't prove a thing.'

'But, Mr Cheel, there is the justices.'

'The justices?' Cheel was puzzled. 'You mean judges and magistrates and so forth?'

'The justices and the honesties and the avoiding of all defraudings.' Braunkopf looked more sombre than ever, so that Cheel's heart sank again. 'You must not disremember the puttikler high ethical –'

'Yes, yes – of course.' Cheel was impatient and rash. 'But I assure you the woman has no title to the things. There's a document to prove it. Her case wouldn't last a day.'

'A document?' Braunkopf's eyes had narrowed. 'That is better, yes – much better. The getting down to copper nails, no?'

'Precisely so.' This one had taken Cheel only a moment. 'As I explained to you, my instructions don't allow of my being very specific about the whole course of events that has brought the Wamba paintings, quite unharmed, to England. But this docu-

90

ment is another matter. Sebastian Holme, you see, sold the lot. And I have the receipt he gave for the money.'

There was a pregnant silence. Braunkopf, who was still on his feet, employed them to transport him with an unnerving noiselessness two or three times up and down the room. He had a waddling motion, Cheel decided, that would make the fortune of a simple mechanical toy.

'The plot sickens, my goot Cheel.' Braunkopf had oscillated to a halt again. 'To just what person, now, would Holme have sold all those pictures? Or perhaps' – he spoke with distinguishable irony – 'that is all confidentials too?'

'Not at all.' Cheel replied confidently. He was extemporizing now – which was of course hazardous and undesirable. He should have thought out this particular ground more carefully beforehand. It hadn't occurred to him that Braunkopf, with the prospect of big money before him, would be quite so wary. But his own confidence had ceased to flicker. He had only to go straight ahead. 'Not at all,' he repeated. 'Kabongo is the name. A wealthy citizen.'

'Some puttikler person called Kabongo bought all those pictures?'

'Just so. A supporter of Mbulu and the RIP, I gather. Holme, you remember, had some idea of arranging his work in an exhibition in honour of Ushirombo. Kabongo paid up simply to put a spoke in that wheel, as you might say. And then, of course, there was the false story of their all having been burnt in the hotel, and so on. It's complicated and obscure – as Mrs Holme would find to her cost if she started an action.'

'You met this Kabongo, Mr Cheel?'

'No, no – nothing of the kind. In fact, Kabongo perished.'

'Perished?'

'When the Wamba State Ballet got a little out of hand. The company was very pro-Ushirombo, you know. To speak quite confidentially, the *prima ballerina* had been Ushirombo's mistress. He's a great favourer of the arts.'

'And this perisher Kabongo, Mr Cheel, conveyed the paintings lawfully to another party?'

'Well, that's where the record turns obscure – and confidential, as I said. The point is that they passed out of Holme's estate.'

'It is a point, yes.' Braunkopf considered. 'And the moneys? Just what did Mr Kabongo pay?'

'Two hundred pounds.'

'Two hundert pounts!' Over Braunkopf's face there passed a fleeting expression of pain. Cheel was uncertain whether this was occasioned by the paucity of the sum named or the indifferent plausibility of his whole recital. And now Braunkopf was stretching out the crudely articulated chunk of dough that served him as a hand. 'The receipt,' he said. 'It requires the careful inspectings, yes? This time, an expertise will be correk. By an authoritarian on handwriting, no?'

'Oh, most certainly.' Involuntarily, Cheel had backed away. 'But I don't carry the thing about with me, of course. It's much too vital a document for that. Naturally, I've lodged it at my bank.'

'We go there now.' Braunkopf appeared to look round for his hat and coat. 'At the Da Vinci, my goot Cheel, we strike while the iron is ripe. Always we cut the grass from under our feet damn-quick.'

'The bank will be shut by now.' This assertion, at least, was unchallengeable, and Cheel was thankful for it. The receipt for £200 given to Mr Kabongo did not, at present, exist – any more than Mr Kabongo, for that matter, had ever existed. But that didn't signify in the least. He knew just where, within a few hours, he could have a little writing-paper printed with the apparent letter-head of the Wamba Palace Hotel. Moreover at one of those shops where moronic persons buy foreign stamps to stick in albums he could probably pick up something that would lend further verisimilitude to a document. And the late Sebastian Holme, fortunately, was available to sign anything of the sort at any time. 'You must see it, of course,' he said lightly. 'And have it examined by an expert, side by side with known writing of

92

Holme's, if you think it desirable. Probably you're right. Yes, I'll drop in with it some time.'

Braunkopf nodded – rather absently, Cheel discerned with relief. Some further aspect of the situation seemed now to be occupying his mind. He walked over to the Quirico, studied it, and gave a small sad sigh. He might have been reflecting that, after all, Mr Kabongo and Cardinal Borgia (to say nothing of Marchese Lorenzo and Conte Cosimo di Medici) were very much birds of a feather. Then he moved back to Holme's picture, 'Clouded Leopards Playing'. He stared at it in a puzzled way for a long time. Once more, Cheel felt uneasy. For a moment he considered the disturbing notion that Braunkopf was one of those legendary dealers of a preternatural acuteness, from whom nothing whatever can be hid. But this was not possible. Braunkopf, after all, was fundamentally absurd.

'I will be fred with you, my dear Cheel.' Braunkopf had turned back to the visitor and was making one of his expansive two-handed gestures.

'You will be what?'

'There must be puffik fredness between us, no? Goot! I divulge, then, that only yesterday I have a most puttikler urgent inquiry one top American collector.'

'For a Sebastian Holme?'

'Exackly that, Mr Cheel.' Braunkopf nodded solemnly. Then he tapped the stretcher of 'Clouded Leopards Playing'. 'It would be a start, yes?'

'Rather a good start, I'd imagine.'

'Fifty-fifty.'

There was a long silence – chiefly occupied by Cheel in summoning strong reserves of astonishment and outrage.

'Come, come, Braunkopf,' he said. 'We mustn't waste time on unrealistic propositions. But I'm perfectly prepared to let you have 25 per cent. Mind you, there are going to be a lot of these paintings.' He frowned to himself, wondering whether this had been an unfortunate choice of words. 'At that commission, you'll make a small fortune before you're finished. And it will be the second fortune that Sebastian Holme has brought your way.'

'Fifty-fifty.'

'This is really insulting, Braunkopf. It's what a shady dealer would suggest in arranging some thoroughly underhand business. I'm afraid I must go elsewhere.'

Braunkopf hadn't blinked. But he had turned back to the painting.

'*That* is shady,' he said softly.

'We will say no more.' Cheel was reaching for his gloves. 'You have made a most outrageous –'

'Such tender shadows, Mr Cheel. A *chiaroscuro* worthy of Caravaggio. Again I will be fred with you. It is a masterpiece.'

Cheel was astonished. It was almost as if Braunkopf had achieved some genuinely aesthetic response to Holme's picture. But this, of course, was impossible. The fellow was a mere tradesman.

'You've begun to talk sense,' Cheel said, pushing his gloves away again. 'So let's consider the share-out realistically.'

'The share-out?' Braunkopf appeared placidly surprised. 'But that is settled. You will find that it is settled, my goot Cheel. Fifty-fifty.'

Cheel's indignation was now genuine. But, equally, his intelligence was at work. And his intelligence told him when he was beaten.

'Very well,' he said. 'Fifty-fifty. And now to fix it.'

Again Braunkopf looked at 'Clouded Leopards Playing'.

'So authentink!' he murmured. 'So strange!'

16

It was in a mood of tolerable satisfaction that Mervyn Cheel presently left the Da Vinci Gallery. Braunkopf's terms were, of course, outrageous; Cheel felt that he would never again listen to the words 'fifty-fifty' – or even 'half-and-half' – without wincing.

Nevertheless there were mitigating considerations. The more Braunkopf stood to gain, the likelier he was to proceed vigorously with the project. Being merely a vulgar commercial man, he would instinctively balance hazards against profits. The larger the possible profit, the less timorous would the proprietor of the Da Vinci be.

Moreover, Cheel reflected, he himself secured a considerably greater margin of safety by working through Braunkopf. The fellow knew all the tricks and channels of the trade, and it was unlikely that he would be badly caught out. Not indeed, that there was anything illegal, anything that could land you positively in the dock, about the whole affair. The only acts of forgery involved were Sebastian Holme's upon his brother's cheques. The pictures to be sold as by Holme were by Holme. It was true that the Director of Public Prosecutions, if through any conceivable misfortune apprised of all the facts, would turn over in his head such terms as False Pretences, Conspiracy, and Fraud. But bringing any such charge would be a tricky business about which that disagreeable personage might well think twice.

And there was another satisfactory consideration as well. A larger share for Braunkopf didn't have to mean a smaller share for Cheel. It need only mean a decidedly smaller share for Holme. This was a matter to which Cheel had already given careful thought. And the more he considered it, the less did it seem to him that Holme need receive any appreciable share at all.

Of course the man must have his keep. It would be injudicious to scant him of reasonably nutritious food. There was no reason why he should not command a regular supply of beer – and even perhaps an occasional bottle of gin. But what more did he need? For that matter, what more had he shown any disposition to ask for? Putting this question to himself as he climbed into the Rolls, Cheel positively felt within himself a gush of warm affection for Holme. For weeks now the man had shown no flicker of interest in anything but standing in that attic and painting all day. The passion with which he had addressed himself to calling back into being 'Mourning Dance with Torches' and

95

'Fishing Cats at Pool' was exceeded only by the indifference with which he had then appeared to regard them. It might have been supposed that, convinced as he was that he could paint only as Sebastian Holme and to further the fame of Sebastian Holme, he would at least have wished to hear that these paintings were going where they would be seen and admired by properly informed people. Yet nothing of the sort had seemed to be in his head. As soon as each was finished he had simply tumbled into bed and slept for twenty-four hours. Then he had got up again, sat brooding darkly for a couple of days, and immediately thereafter started furiously on the next job. Nothing – Cheel thought – could be more admirable.

Nor, for that matter, could Holme be much of a nuisance even if he were minded to turn insubordinate He was now much too much in Cheel's power. Driving down Old Bond Street, with an occasional side-glance at opulent shops into which he might now drop confidently at any time, Cheel thought whimsically of those eighteenth-century booksellers who kept in the garrets of Grub Street teams of hack writers compelled to earn their porridge and small beer by turning out a fixed tally of heroic couplets, moral essays, political pamphlets, heroic dramas, by the day, week or month. That was virtually where he had got Sebastian Holme. Holme perhaps didn't realize it yet, but he would certainly do so at any time that Cheel chose to turn on the heat. The man was, in fact, a slave. Having reduced a painter of genius to such a status tickled Cheel very much. It was amusing. It was so amusing that he felt an appetite for more amusement here and now.

As a consequence of indulging himself with this mood (one not, perhaps, wholly commendable from a moral point of view, but which yet by no means renders our hero very singular among his fellow-mortals) Cheel found himself once more thinking of Burlington House. It was the time of year (he again reminded himself) at which an amazing diversity of bad and mediocre painting was on view in the rooms of the Royal Academy in that compendious palace of learning and the arts. There would be a certain malicious pleasure to be extracted from a stroll round.

And, of course, there was his further campaign against Rumbelow. He remembered his proposal to collect a little more material for that.

As he had expected, it proved possible to park in the courtyard. He swung in neatly, indeed, just before the President of the Royal Society – but as the President was driving a Mini-Minor it was proper enough that he should be left to edge in where he could. Cheel climbed the steps, showed his ticket, and entered the Exhibition.

As usual here, it was difficult to decide where to start laughing. There were the inept productions on the walls; there were the extraordinary people who thought to edify themselves by going round looking at them. Before the pictures, Cheel told himself, it was incumbent upon him to exercise, in the last analysis, a charitable restraint. There was such a virtue as compassion, after all. And it was a virtue, as it happened, that could be deployed very effectively in print. The strictly *pitiful* character of one or another artist's labours was a theme that had frequently stimulated him to an amusing quarter-column.

Nevertheless – he mused, as he began to perambulate among the highly varnished ladies, the company directors with their cigars, the dons with their beastly pipes, the red-faced mayors with their hands manufactured out of sausages, the appalling nudes so evidently painted in a hospital for diseases of the skin, the flat and watery English landscapes – nevertheless a brave scorn was incumbent on him as well. For was he not – as well as a distinguished critic – virtually the pioneer of abstract pointillism? Unlike the wretches exhibiting on the walls around him, he had followed the hard, dry light of art to the end, and never made an iota of concession to public taste. That, and that alone, was why nobody had ever paid the slightest attention to his work. But it was *there* (in packing-cases mostly), and time would vindicate it. It was true that he had been constrained, from time to time, to expedients of dubious dignity in his pursuit of a mere livelihood. He was not without some sense (he told himself) of the dyer's hand. Yet his heart was pure – as the hearts of all the other really great (and often unacknowledged) artists had been. One day his small masterpieces would be assessed at their true worth – and it would be a day when all this rubbish sprawled around him would have perished utterly.

Thus did Mervyn Cheel, continuing his stroll through the rooms of the Royal Academy of Arts, commune with himself as a soul apart. It is very possible that the profane vulgar would have regarded him as a shade mad. They might even have called him a humbug. But here – so far as this particular set of persuasions was concerned – they would have been wrong. His vision of himself was something he held on to with tenacious conviction. It would have been very terrible to Cheel, very terrible *indeed*, to have to succumb to the sort of employment whose fruits he now conceived to be hung around him.

Nemesis (if Nemesis had any disposition to be bothered with Cheel) might well have thought to bear this in mind.

And the people in Burlington House (Cheel had frequently remarked this) were quite as absurd as the pictures. In fact you might say that there were two independent series of exhibits. For example, there were the women of a kind that meet each other in tea-shops. Considerable numbers of them seemed to have the habit of meeting here too. They were to be observed working in labour-saving couples, the first of the partners having the job of looking at the paintings and the second doing all the reading aloud from the catalogue. These women muttered. But there were others – rural rather than urban in suggestion – who talked in loud voices, pointing the while at this canvas or at that with the air of stock breeders at an agricultural show; one had to conceive them as walkers in ancient ways, 'doing' the Academy as their parents or grandparents had done. Then there were sundry small uniformed unfortunates, part of whose precious half-term holiday (one imagined) was being immolated on the altar of aesthetic indoctrination by stupid mothers or bullying aunts. There were elderly men of lavishly cultivated external distinction who must be (Cheel had always supposed) the R.A.s and A.R.A.s themselves, snooping jealously round to see if one or another colleague's exhibits had found a buyer. And there were also (this was really strangest of all) small gangs of art students, attired with a scruffy flamboyance and characterized by a drifting and jostling gait. Perhaps their attendance was compulsory: indeed, there could be no other rational explanation of it.

Charitably entertaining himself with such observations and reflections as these, Cheel took his stand at length in front of the exhibits from which he designed that his principal diversion was to be obtained. These, of course, were the offerings perpetrated by the abominable Rumbelow. The old dotard (as, indeed, he had intimated) was still celebrating the British Way of Life – having been commissioned, it appeared, to produce further enormous murals on the theme. It was a couple of sketches (themselves very large) for these, together with a number of studies of detail, which could be inspected now. Consulting his catalogue, Cheel was surprised – and even a little startled – to notice that the country for which these laboured fatuities were destined was none other than Wamba itself. It was a circumstance he must have quite failed to remark or remember upon the occasion of his brush with Rumbelow's previous offerings in the series. The Palace of Industry for which they were commissioned must presumably have been in existence during the régime of 'Field-Marshal' Mbulu, however little that warrior had been interested in the furtherance of the arts. And Professor Ushirombo must be carrying on with it.

There was something faintly disturbing to Cheel in the coincidence of this tie-up between the activities of Rumbelow and Sebastian Holme. At the same time, there was a certain piquancy in it. Cheel addressed himself with renewed zest to the amusement of finding something really funny to write about Rumbelow's latest efforts. True (he reminded himself) it would have to be a species of *esprit de l'escalier*. When dealing with a ruffian who described himself as not a litigant but a duellist, it would be prudent (as he had earlier resolved) to aim his own shafts from beyond a barrier at least as substantial as the English Channel.

But the dictates of prudence are not always harkened to by large and generous minds. To this the events of the next ten minutes were to bear ample testimony. Yet what happened would not have happened but for the coming together of two facts. Cheel was still in a mood of some elation resulting from the prosperous turn which his affairs had taken and were likely to continue to take. And Cheel had found a present audience for his wit.

The first of Rumbelow's two large sketches was called simply 'Automation'. It represented the interior of a factory in which processes clearly so to be described were going ahead in a big and intricate way. Far more detail was represented than would commonly be found in a preliminary affair of this kind. It gave evidence of the most meticulous calculations and must have been achieved with great labour. The thought of the yet greater toil and sweat that would be required to produce the vast painting that was to be based on it made Cheel feel positively ill. And what made it so particularly awful was (to Cheel's mind) the totally uninspired and (as one might say) triumphantly anaesthetic character of the whole thing. In short, it was the miserable Rumbelow all over.

And it was now that Cheel became aware of an audience: a potential audience. It wasn't large, and it wasn't exactly distinguished. It was, in fact, a couple of the tea-shop women. One, sure enough, had her nose in a catalogue. And the other had her nose in Rumbelow's picture – so much in Rumbelow's picture that she might be smelling whatever oily smells automation may be supposed to produce. Both women appeared to be perplexed. They looked as if they had been brought up on the art of Sir Edwin Landseer – or at most on the bilious females of Sir Edward Burne-Jones. What might be called Industrial Art was beyond them. Still, they were seekers after light. And Cheel was suddenly prompted to supply it. He stepped forward with a bow.

'May I have the pleasure,' he asked, 'of offering an explanatory word?'

17

'You must understand,' Cheel pursued, courteously but in-
structively, 'that the title refers not merely to the scene represented, but also to the method by which the representation has
been achieved. The manufacturer, Mr Rumbelow (who happens
to be a very old friend of mine, by the way), is among the most
notable pioneers of Electronic Art.'

The two women glanced at each other uncertainly. They were
doubtful about the propriety of letting themselves be spoken to by
a male stranger. But Cheel was a person of gentlemanlike deport-
ment and address, and Burlington House, after all, is a place
where a certain bold Bohemianism in manners is admissible.

'How intensely interesting!' one of the women said.

'Mr Rumbelow's notice was first attracted by the spectacle
of what is called Action Painting or *Tachisme*. This, as you
know, is achieved by splashing or dribbling paint on canvas.
What Mr Rumbelow observed was that it seemed a needlessly
messy and laborious craft. He felt his sense of efficiency to be
challenged, and he set his skill as an electronic engineer to work.
Very soon he had perfected a simple machine. The operator
need do no more than sit at an instrument panel. Simply by
depressing a switch, a large and elaborate Action Painting could
be produced virtually instantaneously. The saving in artistic
man-hours was enormous.'

The woman with the catalogue was covertly consulting it. She
must be seeking some confirmation in print of these extraordinary disclosures. Her companion, however, was of a less ungener-
ously sceptical temperament.

'Ah, yes,' she said. 'Of course I've heard of it. But I haven't
actually seen anything done that way before.'

Cheel had to disguise a cackle of laughter as a dignified
cough. Several more people had now gathered around him. He

101

didn't observe them very clearly, but they contributed, somehow, to his own sense of the enormous funniness of his joke.

'But the exhibit before us now,' he went on, something of the tones of a guide-lecturer coming into his voice, 'represents a different order of achievement. Only a technologist as brilliant as Mr Rumbelow could have hoped to bring it off. You will see at a glance that a manufactured article like this, if it had to be made by hand, would involve the most monotonous and soul-destroying labour. And remember, please, that this is only a preliminary design for something much larger, and to be realized in even more overwhelming detail. An unassisted human being could hardly hope to achieve it while retaining his sanity – and certainly not if he were a person of any imagination or sensibility. But Mr Rumbelow has once more risen to the occasion.'

Cheel paused impressively. Actually, his invention was beginning to fail – and moreover he was wondering just how he was going to bring his turn to a close. There were now more than a dozen people gathered around him, and in the attitude of some of them he sensed a certain disapproval. What if somebody called an attendant, or even a functionary of a superior order? He thought he heard a female of the landed-gentry contingent say 'Turn him out', and even the more credulous of the two women constituting his original audience was now looking suspicious. Such was his intrepidity of spirit, however, that these inauspicious circumstances only spurred him on.

'Notice,' he said, 'the unbroken brick wall that is a notable feature of the design. It has been calculated that the full-scale version of the picture destined for Africa will call for the accurate reproduction of eleven million, forty-seven hundred thousand, twelve hundred and eighty-two individual bricks. One single operation on the part of the computing and other devices in Mr Rumbelow's electronic machine will place these precisely in position on the canvas, at the same time observing the strictest canons of both linear and aerial perspective. And now a brief biographical note. My old friend's achievement – I refer to Mr Rumbelow – my old friend's achievement must appear the more notable when we consider the highly disadvantageous circumstances of his early life. His mother – perhaps through some grave defect of intellect, perhaps merely on account of the extremely humble walk of life in which she had been brought up – was never able either to read or write. His father, ostensibly a reputable pawnbroker in a small way of business, was in fact an incompetent and unsuccessful receiver of stolen goods. The boy himself, moreover, in addition to suffering from a distressing scrofulous complaint which he has never in fact overcome, was early discovered to be totally colour blind. This circumstance, in itself somewhat disabling in one whose ambition –'

Cheel broke off – his words suddenly strangled in his throat. Hard by, there had been a roar of rage. It came from a member of his audience who was none other than the evil Rumbelow himself.

There was but one course open to Mervyn Cheel in this hideous situation, and that course he immediately took. Not Hector himself, pursued by the stern Achilles thrice fugitive about Troy wall, made better speed than did Cheel in the direction of the turnstiles of the Royal Academy. Nor did he at all stand upon the order of his going, so far as the minor convenience of others was concerned. In fact he had to knock down two of the wretched children who were being dragged round the Exhibition, and was further constrained to give an intrusive old gentleman a vigorous shove in the face. An imaginative observer of the scene might have expected the pink-coated Masters of Foxhounds (of whom there was the usual quota on the Academy's walls this year) to scramble out of their frames with cries of *Tally-ho* and *Gone Away*.

Cheel might well have made good his escape at once, but for one circumstance. His flight was taking place under the influence of an emotion not very compatible with clear thinking, or even clear seeing. To his fancy at least, Rumbelow's pursuing breath was hot upon his neck – so that he was (to put it quite frankly) pretty well blind with terror. Pounding past the ladies who purvey catalogues and picture-postcards, he retained a dim vision of how one gets *in* to the Royal Academy, and none at all of how one gets *out*. But at least he glimpsed one door through which it was possible to tumble. It bore the inscription *Gentlemen*. Through this he bolted. He found himself instantly in the arms of somebody who was presumably attempting to emerge. It was, he supposed, an attendant. And to this attendant, in his extremity, he addressed an agonized appeal.

'Save me!' Cheel panted. 'Save me, save me!' he contrived breath enough to scream. 'A maniac! Running amuck! Oh, save me, if you can!'

'Steady, old boy, steady.' The voice was not that of an attendant. 'Bit of trouble, eh? Ha-ha! In there, and I'll see you through.'

Cheel felt himself propelled firmly through a door which was then closed on him. He sank down, sobbing. His perambulation of the rooms of the Royal Academy had ended up in what was perhaps the Royal Academy's smallest room of all.

'No, no – nobody here.' He heard the voice of his preserver speaking in large and jovial surprise. 'Yes, a fellow did dash in. A thief or something, eh? Bobbed out again. Out of the building by now, I'd say. Find a copper, if I were you, sir. Deuced sorry, eh? Would have nabbed him, if I'd known.'

A door banged. There was silence. Cheel rose rather unsteadily from the object upon which he had collapsed, opened the door, and peered out. About the voice of his preserver there was something that had brushed his memory even in the midst of his panic. Now, at a single glance, he remembered. This was the man, corpulent in figure and crude in conversation, to whom he owed what champagne he had got upon the occasion of the Sebastian Holme Private View at the Da Vinci Gallery.

18

'Well, well, well!' It was instantly apparent that the corpulent man had lost nothing of his ebullience during the intervening weeks. 'Having a bit of a lark, old chap? Jolly good fun!'

Cheel acquiesced in this description of his late activities. It was with some such notion, after all, that he had entered upon them. And at least the maniac Rumbelow was gone. Perhaps he was pounding down the length of Piccadilly by now, howling for Cheel's blood.

'Simply a fellow with a kind of *idée fixe*,' Cheel said vaguely. 'Has a sense of grievance, or something. I always try to avoid him. That's why I was just slipping out of his way. But thanks a lot, old chap.'

This expression went down well with the corpulent man. It also seemed to stir his memory. He laid a heavy hand on Cheel's shoulder.

'Long time since we met – what?' he asked. 'Deuce of a long time since we lived it up together, eh? Not since St Tropez, I'd say. How's dear old Meg?'

'As a matter of fact, you and I ran into each other not all that long ago at a picture show. At the Da Vinci Gallery.' Having nothing to report about Meg, Cheel said this as the first thing that came into his head.

'So we did!' The corpulent man was delighted. 'And you came out with Debby and me and had a bite at the Caprice.' The corpulent man, whose recollections seemed to be conducted singularly at random, was more delighted still. 'Dear old boy!' he said. 'I wish I could remember what I called you in those golden days.'

'Mervyn,' Cheel replied. He had lately been discovering a reluctance too readily to reveal his identity to the world on casual acquaintance.

'Mervyn, to be sure. And I'm still old Duffy, you know – ha-ha!' The corpulent man, who had presumably been drinking, was now cheerfully pawing Cheel's back. 'What about a quick one?' he asked. 'We'll go out and find Debby and Wuggles – and old Meg, if she's here.'

'Meg isn't here,' Cheel said. He was now wondering how he was going to get away from this mildly pestilential – even if lately providential – person. 'And I'm afraid –'

'By Joye! It was at that fellow Sebastian Holme's show, wasn't it?' The man calling himself Duffy accompanied this fragmentary command of truth by turning his pawing into a vigorous slap between the shoulder-blades. 'That's why we're here now – Debby and me. And Wuggles. Particularly Wuggles.'

'Because of Holme?' Cheel, puzzled, had pricked up his ears. 'But there aren't any of Holme's things here in Burlington House.'

'Of course not. They're damned scarce. That's why I snapped one up at that exhibition. Sure to show growth, you know – assets like that. I aim at a whole portfolio of them. Not Holmes, of course. The issue's exhausted, as you might say. Oversubscribed in a week, eh? But fellows of the same sort. Now, let's collect the crowd.'

Duffy led the way out of the place of retirement in which this colloquy had taken place. Cheel followed with caution. Nor did he immediately bolt on seeing that the coast was clear. That instinct which had of late been so brilliantly guiding his affairs was whispering to him that – just possibly – there was (once more) something in this for *him*.

'Dash it all, where *are* Debby and Wuggles?' Duffy was looking about him in amiable impatience. 'What's the good of having a wife, eh, if she won't wait while a fellow's in the loo? But Wuggles will have dragged her off to see this whatever-it-is. Affair by a fellow called Rumbelow. Being done for the godless place that chap Holme worked in. Wamba, eh? Terriory' Wuggles comes from, you know. Lived there for years. That's why he's interested.'

A strong light of recollection suddenly shone upon Cheel. He remembered, in fact, his recent reading in the newspaper paragraph called Wamba-Wamba Diary.

'Would the real name of – um – Wuggles be Wutherspoon?' he asked.

'It damned well would. I knew you must know Wuggles. All good men know Wuggles. And there they are!' Duffy seized Cheel by the elbow, and propelled him in the direction of a man and woman who were emerging from a farther room. 'Debby – Wuggles,' he shouted, 'here's old Mervyn. We'll all go out and have a spot.'

Mr Wutherspoon (or perhaps, Cheel thought, he was Sir Wuggles Wutherspoon) responded to this informal introduction without cordiality. He was older than Duffy, and a great deal older than Debby; his expression was melancholy; his complexion was of an order which made Cheel want to back away, so powerfully did it answer to his notion of what must be the effect of yellow fever. Nevertheless Wutherspoon looked tough. Indeed, he would have to be called desiccated. In the wilds of Wamba, one felt, he might have been two or three times in and out of some communal *bouillon* pot without ever having very notably contributed to the nutritional needs of the natives.

Debby was different. Cheel felt drawn to her, since she would – so to speak – pinch superbly. But there seemed no immediate sign that she felt correspondingly drawn to him. She was looking at him silently and with disdain. She powerfully suggested one of the larger cats that has gone temporarily off its feed.

'You remember Mervyn at St Tropez,' Duffy was saying. 'And you remember his wife; you remember Meg.'

'Ah, Meg! *Tell* me about Meg.' Debby uttered these words much as if the normal function of language was unknown to her. They were used merely to intimate to anybody who cared to listen that the main emphasis of her own interests lay in an emotional rather than any strictly intellectual direction. This was achieved chiefly by huskiness, but what might be called a

107

gluey quality was also at work. Cheel felt almost giddy. A more intimate inspection than was feasible in Burlington House, he felt, would surely discover her to be with Cupid's amorous pinches black. But, meanwhile, he had to deal with Meg. If he was going to hang on to these absurd people long enough to get a little useful low-down on Wamba from Wutherspoon, he must deal with Meg firmly and now. He might manage to sustain for a little some imaginary sojourn in St Tropez on his own account. But he certainly couldn't drag through such a fantasy an imaginary wife as well.

'Ah, Meg,' he said. 'I must be quite frank with you. Old friends, eh?' This clearly commended itself so highly to Duffy that Cheel took care to side-step smartly by way of avoiding another slamming on the back. 'Meg and I have broken it up. It just didn't do.'

'Ditched your wife?' It was Wutherspoon who snapped this out. 'Quite right. Infernal nuisance. He travels the fastest who travels alone. One of the poets said that.'

'We were greatly attached to each other,' Cheel continued with dignity. 'Debby and old Duffy' – he got this out with difficulty yet with assurance – 'must recall us as a devoted couple. But there was a certain – um – incompatibility.'

'Rubbish!' Wutherspoon said. 'One woman's no different from another. A rag and a bone and a hank of hair. Same poet. No offence to Debby, I hope.'

'So the subject is naturally a painful one. I'd rather not talk about Meg at all.' Cheel said this with the utmost firmness. He was thinking that he didn't at all care for Wutherspoon. Indeed – it occurred to him – the total of people for whom he didn't at all care had been mounting rapidly of late. On the whole, the Holme affair was introducing him to disagreeable characters all round. And disagreeable characters were his particular aversion. However – he reflected – it was undeniably in a good cause.

'Drinks,' Duffy reiterated cheerfully. 'Drinks, drinks, drinks. All hands to the bar. Out – eh? – out.'

108

'Not drinks. Eats. I'm famished.' Debby said this – and so throatily that the effect was one of wild indecency. Oddly enough, it seemed to be at the leathery-yellow Wuggles that she looked as she spoke. Cheel felt his dislike of this demoted nigger-walloper increase.

'Very well.' Duffy made a sweeping movement towards the turnstiles. 'Just a few rounds first, and then we'll eat in a big way. Old Mervyn owes us a square meal. That snack at the Caprice was on us. And Mervyn won't mind filling Wuggles's trough too, eh? Away we go.'

Not unnaturally, Cheel even in his new-found prosperity had winced a little at this proposal. To make a lavish return for a luncheon wholly barmecidal and illusory went much against the grain. But, once more, the cause had to be remembered.

'Most delightful,' Cheel said – and with no more than an involuntary cackle that was just a shade harsh. 'And I want to hear old Wuggles on Wamba. Nothing he doesn't know about it, eh?'

'Wamba?' It was with an oppressive sombreness that Wutherspoon repeated the name. 'All I can tell you about Wamba will go into three words. Some poet thought them up. Birth, copulation, death.'

'Is that so?' Cheel said stiffly. He was always quick to deprecate coarse language.

'And particularly death. I've spent all my days in the place, and I know.'

'Ah, yes,' Cheel said. The party was now making its way down the broad staircase that leads to the outer vestibule of the Royal Academy. Cheel wondered whether he ought to make a bolt for it, after all. Debby had her attractions, but he saw very little probability of being in a position to set finger and thumb to them. Both the men were unbearable.

'People do die, you know, from time to time,' Wutherspoon continued. 'I agree that the fact is kept pretty dark in this part of the world. Still, it does, I should imagine, leak out. It isn't inconceivable that you'll die yourself – although I doubt whether you've ever entertained the notion.' Wutherspoon gave Cheel an unpleasant sideways glance. 'But in Wamba *everybody* dies Sooner or later, everybody born there *dies*. Can you imagine it And what's more, everybody is aware of the fact. I see I've shocked you.'

Cheel said no more for the moment. Quite as many rounds o drinks as Duffy seemed to envisage, he thought, would be necessary if sitting down at table with these people were to be conceivable. He was even resigned to paying for whole bottle: of gin himself. But at least he might as well give them all the works. And now, when they were out in the courtyard, he had the opportunity to make a start.

'If you care to hop into my car,' he said casually, 'we'll go wherever Debby has a fancy for.'

19

Duffy, like most corpulent men, ate a great deal. Wuggles, like most cadaverous men, ate a great deal too. As the dinner went on, and Cheel mentally totted up the lengthening bill, he reflected that Debby represented the only break in the gloom. In spite of having announced herself as famished, Debby ate very little, and could only have been described as *distraite*. She glanced at her watch much more frequently than was civil in the presence of a host; the look in her eye was far-away; she no longer appeared to take any more interest in Wuggles than she did in Cheel himself. It came suddenly to Cheel that she had remembered something – and that it was something that made her discontented with her present company.

But Cheel's serious business did not lie in speculations like these. During the past weeks he had attempted in various ways to equip himself as a modest authority on Wamba and its people and institutions. But reliable information was hard to come by.

Often one ostensible authority blankly contradicted another. In some ways this was all to the good. The more confused the record, the less likely was anybody effectively to question the story he had himself told Braunkopf, and which Braunkopf would have to pass on in a hush-hush manner to whatever customers came forward for the supposedly recovered – but actually so marvellously re-created! – Sebastian Holmes.

Nevertheless Cheel ought to pick up whatever news out of Wamba he could come upon. And here Wutherspoon was very much his man. Indeed if *Wamba-Wamba Diary* was to be believed, Wutherspoon was the top authority one could find.

'Tell me, Wuggles,' Cheel said casually, 'what is the food like out in Wamba?' The specific topic was not one upon which he felt any curiosity, but it seemed an apposite opening with a man who – at great expense to oneself – was stuffing sixteen to the dozen.

'The food?' It was with an increased moroseness that Wutherspoon repeated the word – much as if here was a subject in all circumstances totally revolting to him. 'There is no food in Wamba.' He appeared to weigh this statement carefully. 'Or virtually none.'

'No food!' Duffy, who had been silent for some time over what he doubtless thought of as his trough, was roused to dismay. 'Dash it all, the chaps must eat something.'

'Occasionally there is a sparse crop of ground-nuts, and in good seasons there may be a little wild cabbage. The swampy territories are a shade better off. A frog or lizard can be bagged from time to time. Of course, the chiefs and their families do not do too badly. They have *boko-boko*.'

'Most interesting,' Cheel said.

'Quite possibly' – Wutherspoon pursued contemptuously – 'you have never eaten *boko-boko*. It's a great delicacy: a species of rather bitter carrot, which has been premasticated by the sacred baboons.' Wutherspoon ingested a further supply of quail in aspic. 'There is something very palatable about *boko-boko*.'

This was the first occasion, Cheel reflected, in which Wutherspoon had uttered in what might be termed a commendatory sense. Perhaps he was mellowing. If so, now was the moment for cautiously pressing forward.

'The country seems to have been making remarkable strides politically,' he said. 'I think you've been a close friend of the present Prime Minister, Professor Ushirombo?'

'A damned scoundrel!' Wuggles was suddenly explosive; it was even possible to imagine that his complexion had become faintly tinged with red. 'Just for a handful of silver he left us. Some poet fellow puts it very well. Just for a ribbon to stick in his coat. I *made* the M A D S, you know. I positively created them as a political voice. The Syndicalists were right out on a limb, I can tell you. Literally, many of them. Too scared to come down from the trees. But I negotiated a *concordat* with the Moderate Advanced Democrats. That did the trick at once. Ushirombo was able to come out of hiding (he'd been peddling bicycles, or some such thing) and seize power. Well'— Wutherspoon savagely speared his last fragment of quail – 'the first thing he did was to run me out of the country. That's why I'm here now – and facing penury into the bargain. Ingratitude, thou marble-hearted fiend. Shakespeare.'

Wamba-Wamba Diary, it appeared, had been a shade out of date. Wuggles's present political affiliation, however, was of very little interest. What Cheel wanted to get hold of was chiefly an authentic narrative of the last hours of the Wamba Palace Hotel. The truth was that he was still haunted by doubts. What had put it into Hedda Holme's head that her husband's pictures had been saved? It was, of course, all to the good that there should be some dark rumour of their preservation going around. But it would be disastrous if they *had* been preserved. So what if Sebastian Holme himself were not a reliable witness? At least it would be reassuring to get confirmation out of Wutherspoon.

'I suppose,' Cheel asked, 'you were closely involved with events on the day of the revolution?'

'Day of the revolution?' Wuggles was puzzled. 'Don't know what you're talking about. Revolutions were going on all the time.'

'I mean the night the mob burnt down the Wamba Palace Hotel. I'm interested, you know, as a painter and as a critic of –'

'*You* a painter!' It was Debby who had broken in with this. '*You* can't be a painter. I *adore* painters!' She yawned, and looked at her watch again.

Unmannerly and offensive as this was, Cheel thought well to ignore it.

'There was the talented young fellow Holme,' he said. 'I gather that he and his brother were in Wamba a good deal – and that a whole collection of his paintings was in fact destroyed in that hotel at the time when he was killed.'

'Quite right!' Pushing away an empty plate with a gesture more robust than refined, Duffy interrupted in his turn. 'As a result, the fellow's pictures are damned scarce. I got one, you know. As Debby's just said, she and I are dead keen on pictures. The nineteen-fifties for Equities, my boy, and the nineteen-sixties for pictures. Take my tip.'

'Ah, those two brothers,' Wutherspoon said. 'Up to all manner of mischief. May have been in with JUMBO, for all I know. The elder of them – name of Gregory, I fancy – got away. T'other one was killed. A painter, did you say? Never had any truck with them. Velvet collar-rolls. Moo and coo with women-folk. One of the poets again.'

'But you must take *some* interest. You and I, after all, have just met at Burlington House.' Cheel was not only puzzled; he was, for some reason, faintly alarmed. 'You went, I gather, to look at the designs of an atrociously bad painter called Rumbelow that have been commissioned for some place in Wamba.' As he spoke, Cheel was aware of a movement beside him. Debby had risen and was wandering away. As both her husband and Wuggles remained ungallantly seated, Cheel did the same. The woman had gone, he supposed, to powder her nose. 'So you

can't be all that uninterested,' he went on. 'Did you actually g[]
and see that show of Holme's at the Wamba Palace?'

For a moment Wutherspoon made no reply to this perfectl[]
civil question. He was studying the menu. Indeed, Cheel coul[]
distinguish clearly that his eye was running down a colum[]
devoted to dishes of a particularly rich and costly order. If h[]
had really been expelled from Wamba into penury, he wa[]
evidently well practised in making the most of a gastronomi[]
windfall. So, for that matter, was Duffy – although Duffy wa[]
presumably deep in the lolly. Cheel continued mountingly t[]
dislike them both.

'See the fellow's pictures?' he said. 'Yes, I suppose so. Ofte[]
dropped into the Wamba Palace of a morning for a peg. An[]
in the evening for a sundowner. Yes, I remember noticing them
come to think of it.'

'What's happened to Debby?' Duffy asked. 'Oughtn't to b[]
spending all that time in the loo. Irritating habit. Got her bette[]
house-trained than that. And she'll miss her kickshaw.'

For a moment the kickshaw distracted Cheel's attention. Th[]
chef had been produced to prepare it; he was flanked on one sid[]
by the head waiter and on the other by the *sommelier* (grasping []
bottle of Green Chartreuse); underlings in sinister profusio[]
stood ranked behind. The dish was some sort of *flambé* affai[]
that Cheel himself detested. *Mon argent est flambé*, he tol[]
himself in a mournful pun. But perhaps he would be able t[]
flog one of the new Holmes quietly to Duffy to tuck away in hi[]
portfolio in place of another wad of Equities. There was comfor[]
in that thought.

'I suppose,' Cheel said to Wutherspoon, 'that they wer[]
undoubtedly all destroyed?'

'All destroyed? Don't know what you're on about.' Wuther[]
spoon, who was concentrating upon the culinary process pro[]
ceeding beside him – and in the particular interest, it seemed[]
that the *sommelier* did his stuff generously – glanced at Chee[]
with irritation. 'I'd have him add a dash of their Champagne[]

114

Cognac, if I were you. 409 on the list. And then a glass of it will go well with the coffee.'

'Capital,' Duffy said. 'Good old what's-your-name!'

'Mervyn,' Cheel said, between teeth suddenly chattering with rage.

'Mervie. I'll call you Mervie. Good old Mervie.' Duffy drained his glass in the expectation of what was to come. He could only have been described as already in liquor. 'And tell him to get out his Hoyo Coronas at the same time. There's not a better six-and-sixpenny cigar in London.'

'I quite agree.' To his own ear, Cheel managed this concurrence with an air of easy authority. He gave the necessary instructions to the head waiter, who received them with every appearance of courteously dissimulated contempt. 'Sebastian Holme's pictures,' he said firmly to Wutherspoon. 'I'm asking you whether, to your own certain knowledge, they were all definitely destroyed?'

'Damned impertinent inquisition!' Wutherspoon produced this with a sudden and flabbergasting roar as he dug a fork savagely into the ruinous concoction before him. 'Duffy, who is this awful little man? What's he doing at our table? Have him put out! Have him taken away!'

'Steady, Wuggles my boy.' Duffy was admonitory but not disturbed. 'This is Mervie, you know. Civil little man I picked up somewhere on the Riviera. Not just one of us, perhaps. But a decent sort of yob, and swimming in the gravy. You should see his bloody car.'

Cheel rose to his feet, gibbering with fury. Then he abruptly sat down again. He realized with horror that both these ghastly men had contrived to get drunk without his noticing it. Perhaps that was why Debby had withdrawn. And now people at the nearer tables were turning and staring. He remembered the rather ticklish exit he had been constrained to make with Hedda Holme from another and less pretentious restaurant. This time, it looked like being worse.

'Put him out!' Wutherspoon shouted again. 'A damned insolent intrusion!' He took a large gobbet of the disgusting *soufflé*, or whatever the thing was. Ingested in such a passion, it ought to have choked him. But its effect was quite different. 'Just quieten down,' he said to Cheel. 'You're in danger of creating a scene, my dear chap. Nobody minds a fellow getting a bit tight. But hold it, old boy. Hold it like a gentleman.'

'Good old Wuggles!' Duffy said. 'Good old Mervie! Good old Debby!' He broke off and looked around him. 'Where the hell *is* Debby?'

This question was answered as he spoke. An enormous figure, liveried in the manner of a door-keeper or linkman, had appeared at the entrance to the restaurant and was now advancing upon the three diners. Cheel took it for granted that they were all about to be chucked out. The man, however, paused beside Duffy, and made a respectful bow.

'Madam's compliments, sir, and she regrets she has had to leave.'

'Had to leave, eh?' Duffy seemed not particularly perturbed. 'Tummy gone wrong, perhaps?'

'No, sir. She sent a message, sir. Something she had remembered. A visit to pay. An overdue visit, she said, to her old governess. With her compliments, sir, as I said.'

Duffy received this communication – which could scarcely have been intended for credence, Cheel supposed – with an amiably dismissive wave of the hand. Then he seemed to recollect himself.

'Mervie, old boy,' he said, 'give this chap half-a-crown – there's a good fellow. No – damn it! – give him five bob. And where's that brandy? We've the night before us.'

20

To revel into the small hours with Duffy and Wuggles was something Mervyn Cheel simply couldn't take. His mature self-knowledge (which has already so variously exhibited itself in this narrative) told him at once that if he made the attempt he would probably end up by committing murder. He therefore worked the lavatory game. That is to say, he withdrew from his companions precisely as Debby had appeared to do; and like Debby he didn't return. Unlike Debby, however, he sent back no message about an old governess, or even about an old tutor. He just collected his hat and coat, and walked out. The perfect simplicity of this manoeuvre pleased him very much – particularly when he reflected that it had left Duffy and Wuggles to face the bill, after all. He had decided that, in the way of information, there was nothing more to be got out of either of them. And as neither of them looked like being good for anything else – or for anything more, say, than an occasional casual drink – they were in the most obvious sense expendable. It was true that they might, upon some future occasion, fall in with him and exact vengeance. They might even deliberately chase him up with that in view. But on the whole this seemed not probable, since they were both so tight that it was unlikely they would preserve any clear memory of what the evening had been about.

It was in very reasonable good humour, then, that Cheel recovered his splendid car and drove home to the comfortable flat with which he had now provided himself. The arduous day could close with the most innocent of pleasures: a hot bath, a night-cap, and a quiet half-hour with a volume chosen at random from his very respectable collection of refined *erotica*.

Unfortunately this plan didn't materialize. He had hardly closed the door behind him when he realized that beneath his good humour an indefinable uneasiness was at work. The feeling

117

was the more unpleasant because he felt that he *ought* to be able to explain it. For some time he mooned about indecisively. He turned on a bath, and then turned it off. He poured himself a drink, and then abandoned it on the chimney-piece. He chose a book, and it didn't seem to tickle him at all. Perhaps, he thought, he was suffering delayed shock from the atrocious behaviour of the savage Rumbelow in Burlington House. Perhaps he didn't trust Braunkopf. Perhaps –

Quite suddenly, Cheel spotted the trouble – the operative trouble at the moment. (There were a good many others, after all, rather ominously prowling on the horizon.) There had been something factitious – something bogus, to use a vulgar expression – about that sudden outburst from the man Wutherspoon when he had been tackled about Sebastian Holme's pictures. At the time, the gross indignity of the expressions then directed at Cheel had obscured this fact from him. But he saw it clearly now. Wutherspoon had been concerned to break off the topic. In other words, Wutherspoon knew something he had been trying to conceal. Could he, conceivably, be possessed of the truth about Sebastian Holme's continued painful drawing of breath in this harsh world? If he were, could he be hoping (as would be only rational, after all) somehow to cash in on his knowledge? He had spoken bitterly of having returned to England in penury. Did he know something that might get him out of it?

Mervyn Cheel prowled up and down, gloomily perpending these questions. He had a baffled feeling that they had got him well into a target area, but that he still hadn't scored a bull's-eye. This irritated him. Glancing around him, he saw, carefully wrapped up in brown paper, the only freshly re-created painting of Holme's that now remained to him. That morning there had been two. But 'Clouded Leopards Playing' was now locked up in the Da Vinci Gallery.

Holme must be given a sharp prodding. This persuasion came to Cheel with a force from which he ought to have taken warning that it wasn't entirely rational. In sober fact, the painter's

118

industry was phenomenal; there were several virtually completed pictures in his attic fastness now; within the week, another had been coming along. These circumstances should have been prominent in Cheel's mind at this moment. It would have been well if he could have realized that Passion was usurping the Rule of Reason in his mind. He had been a good deal harried in the course of the day. He wanted to harry Holme.

Another thought came to him. Within this same past week, Holme had for the first time demanded quite a lot of money. Not, it was true, in any *absolute* reckoning a considerable amount. In fact it had been no more than £50. But what earthly occasion did the man have for even that? When one looked at it in this way, one saw clearly that Sebastian Holme was becoming displeasingly grasping. Not only must he be prodded along. He must also be pulled up.

At this point Cheel remembered that he had certain supplies to deliver to Holme. For their original arrangement had been maintained. Cheel had done all the purchasing of artists' materials, and had delivered them at his own former lodging. Holme oughtn't to be given any excuse for idleness on the pretext of not having received this or that on time. Cheel would go along with these various commodities now. The hour, indeed, was late. But it would do no harm to show Holme that there was no time of the day or night at which he mightn't expect to be kept an eye on.

It is melancholy to have to remark that in all this there might have been detected at play an element of mere and useless fantasy. It was the fantasy of Cheel as Master and Holme as Thrall. If it had come to birth on any specific occasion, that occasion may well have been the moment of Holme's turning from the abstract pointillist creations of his fellow-conspirator with the dispassionate remark that they were pretty average rubbish. At that moment, of course, Cheel would have liked to have possessed some means of taking the young man's hide off his back. And this feeling had conceivably remained with

119

him. Had he, at this present juncture, had mental recourse to his favourite play, he might have reflected that one who proposes to thrive by making his fool his purse (which was precisely his design upon Sebastian Holme) must not, indeed, dull device by coldness and delay – but must have an equal care to go to work tenderly. Cheel didn't go to work tenderly now. He was annoyed. And at this late hour he tumbled out of his flat again, resolved a little to twist the tail of Sebastian Holme.

21

The attic apartment from which Cheel had lately withdrawn, and in which Sebastian Holme now led his industrious and reclusive life, had at one time accommodated the three or four female servants deemed requisite in the London establishment of a solid although not notably prosperous citizen. The citizen had long since departed; the tall house – never other than unbeautiful – had a shabby and disgraced air; its staircase was now the common means of entrance to a warren of unassuming but by no means inexpensive flats.

Cheel parked his car round the corner (for some reason he hesitated to advertise his new splendour in this old haunt) and collected in his arms the various supplies that Holme's present activities required – including a large canvas which was quite soon (Cheel reflected) going to be worth several pounds sterling per square inch. He moved round to the front of the house and observed that its upper parts were in complete darkness. Holme must have gone to bed. This might be regarded as satisfactory, since it no doubt conduced to his working efficiency that he should keep regular and early hours. If he was asleep by eleven there was no reason why he should not be standing before his easel by eight the next morning. And if he was asleep now Cheel would have the satisfaction of waking him up without ceremony.

The windows on the second floor were lit up, however, and

there were sounds suggesting that someone was giving a party. Cheel had never held much commerce with his former neighbours, and he did not expect to meet any of them now. But in this he was mistaken. Just as he climbed the stairs the party began to break up, and several people gave him a perfunctory greeting as they passed. The tenant on the second floor, who went by the name of Binchy, was a sub-artistic character understood to scramble up a living out of scratching designs on glass. Binchy was standing in his doorway, speeding his parting guests. He hailed Cheel now.

'Evening to you,' he said. 'Another whacking canvas, eh? That's the second I've seen you scurrying home with. Quite stepping up your ambitions, aren't you? It will take you the hell of a time to cover a surface like that with all those damned silly little spots.'

This highly offensive manner of referring to the art of abstract pointillism not unnaturally gave marked offence to Cheel, who responded only with a stiff inclination of the head. At the same time it struck him as reassuring that even a close neighbour like Binchy was unaware of the change of tenancy that had occurred. Holme's very existence, it seemed, must be totally unsuspected. It might be a good idea, even at some sacrifice of dignity, to encourage Binchy in his ignorance. Cheel therefore turned round and assumed an affable manner.

'It's certainly not my old style of thing,' he said, tapping the stretcher of the canvas. 'I'm busy at something quite different, as a matter of fact.'

'What's that?'

'Aha!' Despite himself, Cheel gave a cackle of laughter. 'As to that, my dear fellow, I'm not sure that I ought to tell you. I'm not sure, indeed, that anybody will ever quite *precisely* know.' Cheel was about to turn away when he remembered how very rude this nasty man had just been. 'And how are the jolly old lavatory windows and tooth-mugs?' he asked. 'So long.' He gave a triumphant nod, and climbed the next flight of stairs.

The top landing was in darkness. He had to set down his

121

burden and fumble for the light-switch. When he found it, a
flick at it produced no result. Somebody – presumably Holme –
had failed to replace a burnt-out bulb. Moreover the door of the
attic was locked, so that he had to fumble further for a key which
he had sensibly retained. These awkward movements put him
in an ill humour again. He unlocked the door and flung it open.
He found and turned on the light.

'Wake up!' he said, loudly and peremptorily.

But his words had no effect – for the good reason that the
attic was empty.

There could be no doubt of it. The place consisted only of the
one large room. Cheel himself had rigged up a screen which to
some extent demarcated his sleeping from his waking life. But
this, at the start, Holme had torn down and tossed aside. A
glance was enough to confirm the disconcerting fact that
Sebastian Holme had vanished.

For a moment Cheel felt something like hideous panic. He
had, after all, experienced a very trying day, and it is understandable that, for a brief space, his nerve should desert him. What if
Holme – as once in St James's Park – had toyed (this time fatally)
with the impulse to contact the police? Almost for the first time,
it crossed Cheel's mind that if Holme was in *his* power, so,
equally, was he in *Holme's*. If the unaccountable young man
(and he was, distinguishably, that) chose to have a fit of con-
science – or merely elected some rash throwing-over of the
traces – things might turn very awkward indeed.

There was an easel in the middle of the room – and on it, of
course, was a Sebastian Holme in the making. *Unmistakably* a
Sebastian Holme. Cheel shut the door abruptly behind him.
There was a risk (which hadn't before occurred to him) in the
mere fact that, in the person of Binchy, an artist of sorts lived
down below. Other people with some knowledge of painting
presumably frequented his society. Might not any of them
wander up here when the door was open – and be in possession
of sufficient relevant knowledge to find such a picture as this

122

astonishing? Cheel sat down on the couch. An uncomfortably chilly sensation had run down his spine. Holme, he realized, must be given much stricter instructions under the head of what had to be called security. He'd speak pretty stiffly to him as soon as he returned.

But *would* he return? What if he had bolted for good – perhaps having lost his nerve, or perhaps having fled the country in some fit of nostalgia for those exotic parts in which, after all, his authentic inspiration lay?

Cheel looked about him. He might get a clue as to whether or not Holme had departed for good by seeing whether he had taken his belongings with him. But then he virtually didn't have belongings. He had been seeming to make do very happily with the clothes he stood up in, a pair of pyjamas and a toothbrush. Certainly there seemed to be nothing missing from the untidy room. On the other hand – Cheel stiffened – there were several things that hadn't been there upon the occasion of his last visit. There were two large, flat cardboard boxes. There was a crumple of tissue paper and paper bags. Cheel crossed to a cupboard and flung it open. Holme's clothes were hung in it: the only clothes he had hitherto possessed.

With mounting misgivings Cheel inspected the bags and boxes. They all came from a respectable men's outfitter in Regent Street. The larger box had almost certainly contained a ready-made suit. The other might have held shirts, socks, ties and the like. Moreover, under the litter of paper, there turned out to be an empty shoe-box as well. It was only too clear what had become of that £50.

It was a crisis – but a crisis to which Cheel's intelligence responded with the vigour that might be expected of it. If Holme had decided simply to cut and run, and had naïvely provided himself with only such a very moderate sum with which to do so, he certainly wouldn't have spent it on merely togging himself up. The man had the temperament of a feckless Bohemian, but he wasn't a half-wit. He had acted on some impulse that might well be totally irresponsible. But – again – his temperament must

123

have been involved. What, in terms of this, could suddenly have persuaded him to rush out and dress himself up?

Considering this problem, Cheel stumbled on a thought before which he paled and abruptly sat down again. What if Holme had gone off and reconciled himself with his wife? It was true that his regular epithet for Hedda Holme was 'awful', and that occasionally he even used expressions much less printable. Nevertheless his attitude to her was ambivalent. There was, he seemed lurkingly to acknowledge, something to be said for Hedda. Cheel had no difficulty whatever in imagining just what this was.

Cheel contemplated for some minutes the sombre situation at which he had thus arrived. If Holme had suddenly decided that it was time he went out and found himself a woman, he certainly wouldn't have considered it necessary to pay an expensive visit to Regent Street first. But before the thought of Hedda something of the sort seemed possible. Hedda clearly set some emphasis on appearances – and would be doing so more than ever, now that she was so grossly in the lolly. Her prodigal husband might well calculate that she would be more acceptive of him if he didn't turn up smelling of a studio.

Here was a dangerous – indeed dire – state of affairs. Confronting it, Mervyn Cheel would have been more than human if he hadn't, for a brief space, contemplated bolting in his turn. He hadn't of course (he again reassured himself) perpetrated any crime. But crime – or at least fraud –was something on which the law could demonstrably take very unreasonable views. So perhaps he ought to call it a day. Apart from that trifling £50, he had cleared the whole profit on his private sale of the first two Holmes. None of his present splendours had involved the putting down of much spot cash. He found himself thinking about the hour at which his bank opened in the morning, and about a quick run out to London Airport thereafter.

But it was now – need the reader be surprised? – that the essential quality of the man appeared. All was *not* lost, even although the day appeared to have been so. His worst fears

124

might be groundless. Even if they were not, was he not possessed of that quite exceptional degree of intellectual endowment and dexterity of address that is bound to triumph over even the most adverse circumstances? He would stay. He would stay and fight upon the field.

Having arrived at this resolution (and the strong word is here a wholly apt one) Cheel looked at his watch. It was far past midnight; the smallest of the small hours lay ahead. He supposed that he ought to go back to his flat, and return here in the morning. But this, he quickly saw, wouldn't do. To stay and fight meant *literally* to stay. Once he left, he mightn't bring himself to come back again. He couldn't imagine himself climbing all those stairs after breakfast with the knowledge that what he might find at the top would be a couple of detectives from Scotland Yard. No – he must simply sit down and wait. If Holme failed to return within the next few hours he would have to think again.

He walked over to the easel and examined the current re-creating of a lost Sebastian Holme. It was called, he remembered, 'Primal Scene with Convolvulus'. The convolvulus was there, and the primal scene was there too. The latter seemed to be notably outlasting the poet's 'poor benefit of a bewildering minute', since the proliferating tendrils of the flower had wreathed themselves around the bronze and ebony of the lovers' limbs. It might be called, Cheel supposed, an erotic painting; indeed, he wasn't confident that some aged magistrate mightn't be sharked up to disapprove of it. Having nothing with which to occupy himself and thereby distract his mind from its present weight of care, Cheel tried taking 'Primal Scene with Convolvulus' in this direct and simple sense – substituting it, so to speak, for that spell of bed-time reading which he had missed out on earlier that night.

It didn't work. High sexual excitement – for all he knew to the contrary – had gone into the making of the picture. But all that issued from it was a stern command to sacred awe. Uneasy already, Cheel grew still more uneasy before this thing. He even

125

pretended to himself that he had inspected it only to make sure that it had been worked on within the last few hours. For what the point was worth, it had. Holme's flight – if it was flight – had only just begun.

Time wore on. Cheel felt thirsty, but there was nothing to drink in the place except some nauseous coffee powder. He even felt hungry – and the little larder proved to contain two kippers. Two o'clock sounded, and then three. It grew cold. Sometimes Cheel wrapped a rug around himself. Sometimes he got up and stamped about the room. On the canvas the two lovers remained immobile in their long ecstasy.

22

Cheel jerked awake from an abominable dream. They had lashed him tightly to the naked body of Hedda Holme with the cord-like tendrils of some hideous bindweed – a bindweed that at the same time smotheringly extruded a mass of blossoms with a nauseous smell. To struggle was unthinkable, and when he tried to scream his mouth was instantly filled with fleshy petals. Then they cut him free, but only to lead him away to some further torment. And he was still bound: this time in manacles that clanked as he moved. The manacles still clanked when he woke up. But they had become the bottles and metal baskets on a milk-float making its noisy matutinal progress down the street outside.

He struggled out of the chair in which he had dropped asleep, and went over to the big north window. London under its smoky dome was facing another day. Below, there was as yet no life except the milkman's and that of a couple of cats. Opposite, the windows still showed drawn curtains and blinds; only at one of them an old man stood under a naked light, shaving himself with a cut-throat razor. It was a world in *grisaille*, without a note of colour in sight. Here, Cheel thought, was a reality as dreary as his late nightmare had been terrifying. England (it

126

came to him) was getting him down. He could take no more than a few further months of it. He must make his pile, and go.

'Well, I'm blessed – fancy finding you around at this hour!'

Cheel swung round as he was addressed. The truant Holme had entered the room. He was in new clothes that had gone a little untidy, and he was carrying a bottle of milk and an array of paper bags.

'Had breakfast yet? I suppose not. Plenty for two.' Holme grinned amiably. 'Just light that stove affair, and put on the kettle and the frying-pan. I'm dropping into the bog.' Holme put down his provisions and vanished.

Cheel did as he had been told. He was feeling a little dazed. Holme's manner had been totally unexpected. For a moment he had thought the man must be tight. But it wasn't that. It was – But Cheel didn't need to tell himself what it was. He had sensed it in a flash.

'Now, that's fine.' Holme was back in the room, and looking lazily round it. He walked to the window, glanced out, yawned, stretched, and turned back to Cheel. 'Well,' he said cheerfully, 'I thought I would. And I did.'

'Did what?'

'Had her, my dear man. The data given, the senses even. But not *all* the senses. I dropped off to sleep in the course of the proceedings – it's a nice thing to do, don't you think? – and when I woke up I was damned hungry. I could have *eaten* her. But, of course, that would have been wasteful. So we're going to eat now.' Holme strode over to the stove. The movement took him past 'Primal Scene with Convolvulus', and he paused to gaze at it. 'Yes, by God!' he said. 'And – do you know? – I'd almost forgotten it.'

Cheel felt rage rising within him. It was rising from somewhere very deep indeed. He was aware that it might irrationally and disastrously master him. And as yet he hadn't at all got the measure of this crisis. It mightn't *be* all that of a crisis, for that matter. But he must, he simply must, keep cool.

'Mind the eggs,' he said. Holme had dumped down one of his

paper bags so carelessly that there had been an ominous crack.

'Fidgety Cheel, fretful Cheel – one can't, you know, make an omelet without breaking them.' Holme proceeded to enforce this by opening another packet, dropping a blob of butter into the frying-pan, and rapidly breaking and stirring in something like a dozen eggs. 'Make some of that coffee-stuff, will you? Give you something to do. Luckily I brought half-a-dozen rolls.'

Could it – Cheel asked himself – *could it possibly* have been Hedda? Mercifully, he felt free to doubt it. It wasn't that he didn't believe the young brute perfectly capable of speaking in that unbearably coarse way of sleeping with his own wife. It certainly wasn't that he judged the Holmes' cordial mutual detestation any bar to their tumbling into bed together if they felt the itch for it. It was rather a conviction that, if Holme had managed to lay his wife again, she wouldn't have thereafter let him go all that quickly.

No – there was nothing in question but some low, casual adventure. It wouldn't, of course, do. He couldn't let Holme cut out of his work like this to go off wenching. It was a waste of time, for one thing. For another, it probably diverted into useless channels physical energies that ought to be bent on extracting sensations only from pigment. Above all, it was dangerous. Any little tart, professional or amateur, about London might prove to be Sebastian Holme's Delilah. Until his task was finished, until every lost picture in the Wamba catalogue was in being again, nothing more of this sort must occur. Even so, it would be prudent to discover something a little more specific about last night's adventure. With this in view, Cheel gave a few minutes to making coffee in as relaxed a manner as he could. He even looked at the rolls and made some cordial remark about them. Indeed, after his chilly vigil he would be glad enough to get his teeth into a couple of them. And the omelet – which was in fact an enormous dish of scrambled eggs – was beginning to look uncommonly palatable.

'Who was it?' he presently asked, with an air of friendly conspiracy.

'Who was who?'

'This girl you've had a night out with.'

'Ah, that would be telling.' Holme again produced his cheerful grin. It was almost – Cheel reflected with distaste – as if this cursory copulation had effected some quite disproportionate release of tension in the young man; had produced, indeed, something very close to a change of personality. Even Holme's body seemed to have taken on, for the time, a new ease and a new poise. This was the Sebastian Holme, Cheel had to suppose, who had to so agreeable an end locked up Professor Ushirombo in a privy.

'And it would be telling,' Holme went on, 'to no purpose. Not your line, Cheel. All you need is a rubber woman, with a five-year guarantee against pinching. They can be had in Port Said. I'll get you a whopper one day.' He clattered a couple of plates down on the table. 'Eat up,' he said. 'Eat up, and then explain yourself.'

Cheel had no ability to eat up. His rage was such that his lower jaw appeared to be conducting a private epileptic fit of its own. What was unbearable was that Holme didn't appear to feel that he had been insulting; he had the air of simply having made genial reference to established fact. But, once more, Cheel presently achieved control. He even got down some of the scrambled eggs and took a big bite at a roll. His jaw proved to come more or less all right when thus given plenty to do. And meanwhile he considered in silence just how this young man was to be told where he got off. The expression was a vulgar one, such as would not normally have been admitted by Cheel's fastidious linguistic sense. But it was quite inadequate to the strength of his feelings now.

Holme, whose table-manners were predictably unrefined, had wiped his plate clean with a last fragment of roll.

'That's better,' he said. 'A lot better. Why cannot we as well as cocks and lions jocund be after such pleasures? No reason at all. And they come round again. That's the marvellous thing.'

129

'They do nothing of the sort!' At last Cheel had spoken – more sharply than he had intended, perhaps. But it was a relief to have turned upon Holme, and he went on in the tone that he had begun. 'Let's get this clear. You cut right out of whore-mongering until this job is finished. Then you can get back to Africa, blast you, and fornicate among your damned blacks.'

These strong words – courageous as coming from one whom Holme had once laid out with a nasty right hook to the jaw – appeared to make very little impact. Holme, who had begun to mix himself another mug of the coffee stuff, simply continued to do so. Then he lit a cigarette, and as a polite afterthought offered the packet to Cheel.

'By the way,' he said, 'as soon as your bank opens I want you to drop in and fetch me some cash. Say £500.'

'£500!' Cheel was genuinely outraged. 'And what, may I ask, would *you* be doing with £500? I've named your job. It's to control your lecherous fancy and get on with those pictures.'

'That's the sum I want at the moment, old boy, and that's the sum I intend to have. Perhaps for no better reason than to keep in my pocket. Perhaps to give Mervyn Cheel Esq. a glimpse of where Mervyn Cheel Esq. gets off. Get? A favourite word of Hedda's that. And quite a useful one. Get, Cheel?'

That it should be *Cheel* who was to be told where he got off was a proposition so outrageous to Cheel that he tried to laugh robustly – and succeeded only in producing a disconcerting scream. And at this Holme laughed robustly instead.

'Draw it mild, Cheel,' he said. 'You've been imagining things, you know. Just because I work the way I do – hell-for-leather and all-oblivious for a couple of months – you've taken it into your silly head that you have me exactly where you want me. A harmless drudge, worth no more than a stick and a carrot. Have you a notion, my dear man, of the sort of things I've done and seen, the holes I've fought my way out of, the tables I've turned before now on rascals a damned sight more competent than you? When we first met, you know, I was still in a state of shock about Gregory. He was a very decent chap, as I think I said. Not

130

that you'd understand that. But the point is that here I am as I am, and that sometimes I'll work and sometimes I'll do what I bloody well choose. Any remarks?'

'Yes – several.' Cheel had got to his feet – partly through mere agitation, and partly with some idea that it would be wise to preserve as much physical mobility as possible while this situation rose to its crisis. 'If anybody's been imagining things it's been you. And I'll tell you one of the things you've been imagining. You've been imagining that you are Gregory Holme, and entitled to sign Gregory Holme's name at the foot of Gregory Holme's cheques. Where might that put you? Not, perhaps, where Ushirombo would like to put you – which I suppose to be in the middle of an ant-hill, or something like that. But certainly in one of Her Majesty's prisons for longer than it's at all nice to think of.'

'While Cheel Esq. continues to roll in his rotten Rolls?' Holme laughed more robustly than before. 'Don't think I haven't seen you in it. And a pretty beggar on horseback you look.'

'You can put it in that vulgar way, if you like. But it's the plain fact of the case. There's nothing illegal, you know, in discovering that a man isn't dead. And there's nothing illegal in negotiating the sale of an artist's pictures for him. If that artist happens to have been dead and come alive again – well, that's his own affair.'

'What about the story you told whoever bought "Mourning Dance with Torches"? What about the story you told whoever bought "Fishing Cats at Pool"? What about the story you must be telling now about "Clouded Leopards Playing"? Isn't it plain false pretences to claim that these things were rescued from the Wamba Palace? Come off it, Cheel. We're in this rotten show up to the neck together.'

'You're quite wrong there, Holme. I've put nothing in writing about where the things came from. And no court is going to waste much time over an aggrieved purchaser retailing a yarn he claims was spun to him over a couple of whisky-and-sodas.

It's you who are up to your neck, old boy. I haven't so much as got my toes wet.'

Lighting a cigarette, Cheel paused to give time for this to sink in. He felt that he was recovering his own nervous tone, and that there was now a good chance of nipping Holme's rebellion in the bud. At the moment, it would be best to go off confidently on another tack.

'By the way,' he said easily, 'does the name of Wutherspoon convey anything to you?'

'Wutherspoon?' There was impatience in Holme's voice as he repeated the name. He seemed, in fact, not in the least anxious to break off the battle. 'I remember a Wutherspoon out in Wamba. They called him Wuggles.'

'That's the man. Would you say that he had any interest in art and artists?'

'Oh, definitely. I remember that very clearly. It was an uncommon thing out there. But what has Wutherspoon got to do with our affairs?'

For a moment Cheel made no reply. His recovered poise seemed to have been knocked from under him. He had seldom – sensitive instrument that he was – felt a stronger intimation of trouble from afar. Seconds ago this had been no more than a faint tremor: the dying echo of something obscurely disturbing in the course of his last night's luckless dinner. Now there was not only a tremor but a rumble as well. It was volcanic eruptions rather than earthquakes, he supposed, that began that way.

'You're quite sure?' he asked. 'We are speaking of the same man – a fellow like a mummy that's been given a lick of yellow paint?'

'That's Wutherspoon, all right. Some sort of British government underling who started playing ball with one revolutionary group and another. It didn't pay off, it seems. In fact, he was run out of the place.'

'Exactly.' Cheel had now fallen to pacing restlessly up and

down the room. 'Look here – could Wutherspoon possibly know about you and your brother?'

'What do you mean – know about us?' For some time now Holme had been sprawled on the couch. His posture seemed to Cheel quite insolently that of one who has lately taken an agreeable path to luxurious physical repose. 'Is this another of your feeble notions of bullying me, old boy?'

'It's nothing of the sort. It's something that I'm beginning to think may be serious. *Could* Wutherspoon possibly know that it's you who are alive and Gregory who's dead?'

'He could not. Why should this rotten Wutherspoon be bugging you?'

'I had dinner with him last night. When I tried to ask him a question or two about you and your work he took up the attitude that he couldn't care less. When I persisted he created a diversion by flying off the handle.'

'What rubbish!' Holme laughed contemptuously. 'Anybody might fly off the handle with you. Think what a beastly character you are.'

'I don't like it.'

'Nobody possibly could. It's a *mean* kind of beastliness, if you follow me.'

'I'm not talking about what you think of me. I don't care a damn about that. I'm talking of Wutherspoon's behaviour. I don't like his taking that violently evasive action. It meant something.'

'It means no more than that you're a jittery type, I'd say.' Holme yawned, stretched out his arms, and flexed his wrists in sensuous ease. 'And if it's all you've left to jaw about you'd better go away. I feel like a spot of kip.'

'It's not all, by a long way. I come back to where I started. You may think you're invisible behind that ugly great beard again. But I'm not going to have you risk discovery, all the same – not until your job's completed. You're not going out after that tart again – or any other tart.'

133

'Well, well, well!' Holme had sat up. He seemed genuinely astonished. 'How on earth do you imagine you can enforce your crazy fantasy of discipline? Don't you realize, you funny creature, that your attitude is plain pathological?'

'Don't *you* realize, you idiot, where you stand in this affair?' With what was surely abundant provocation, Cheel was hugely incensed again. 'You haven't got two pence. You haven't got a penny. And I'm your paymaster. Toe the line, or you're down to bread and lard. And now, Holme, I'll leave you to think it over.'

'Do. By all means do.' Holme had got to his feet. Although not gigantic, he was a very powerful young man. 'But I suppose you will have to come back for *that*?' He pointed to 'Primal Scene with Convolvulus'. 'You'll have to come and smuggle it out – and then sell it?'

'Certainly I shall.'

'Very well. When you do come, it will be with that £500. If you arrive without it, I'll give you a thrashing. Not a beating-up – because, you know, I'm quite civilized, really. Just a kid's straight thrashing. But the hell of a one. Now, clear out.'

23

As when thwart winds meet, fear and fury joined battle in the breast of Mervyn Cheel. And on the flank, too, skirmished a small gale of sheer bewilderment. For the Sebastian Holme of this appalling morning was simply not the Sebastian Holme of his first acquaintance. He was not, for example, the Holme who had appeared almost as alarmed as himself upon the occasion of the irruption of the abominable Rumbelow. He was not the Holme who had looked positively hunted whenever there had been mention of his disagreeable wife. But he *was* a Holme – Cheel saw it clearly – who had now got his brother's death and his own flight from Wamba distanced and behind him. More than that, he was a Holme who had started painting again, and was proving himself (so to speak) on canvas. Above all, he was a Holme who had just carried some squalid sexual intrigue to a successful conclusion. It was utterly revolting that so vulgar and trivial an exploit should, in a word, set a man up again. But life (Cheel reflected) is constantly confronting us with such sombre facts as this. One deeply read in its wisdom must accept such murky places as simply existing – and must make his market in them.

'Look here,' he said, 'you'll get your money in the end. But at present it's no good to you. It serves only as a distraction. Look at that £50 I gave you.'

'Gave me?'

'Paid you. Transmitted to you. Whatever you like. All you can think to do is to run out and buy yourself finery – and hold on to five quid for a night with a tart.'

'Cheel you're filthy, too filthy for words.' Disconcertingly, Holme had roared with laughter. 'I've never had a woman for money in my life. I've never seen any sense in it. It's a waste of cash, and must be a waste of woman too – like smothering ordinary, wholesome food in some cheap and nasty sauce. Have you ever thought of manufacturing something like that?'

'I don't see –'

'It just occurs to me that yours would be rather a good name for it. A small bottle of Cheel, please. A bargain today, three-pence off, and a packet of stomach powder thrown in free. Cheel makes happy homes. Cheel for getting down left-overs.'

It was natural that this highly offensive nonsense should leave its quarry unamused. Cheel moved in dignified silence to the door. And then – with weird prescience, as it proved – an obscure uneasiness once more overcame him.

'Well, then,' he said, 'if it wasn't a tart, who was it? How did you get off with her so quickly? It wasn't somebody you'd ever known before?' He looked almost pleadingly at Holme. 'You wouldn't be as insanely irresponsible as that?'

'I do believe that you think it may have been Hedda.' Carefree

135

amusement again overcame Holme. 'But it wasn't. And it was nobody else from my past – or from Gregory's, for that matter. It was just a wench I picked up.'

'A low-class amateur?'

'Not a bit of it. What you might call high-class, if your standards are cheap enough.' Holme frowned. 'No – dash it! – that isn't right. She's dumb and she's vulgar – but I'd call her rather a good sort. And when it came to the really relevant thing –'

'All right,' Cheel said. He certainly didn't want to listen to technicalities. 'Now forget her.'

'I'm not sure that I mean to. I only ran into her, you see, a week ago.'

'You mean you've been going out quite regularly?'

'Why the hell shouldn't I? Not that I have, very much. But I did dodge out to see some sculpture by a chap I rather admire. It's in a little gallery in Soho. And there this wench was. Saying she adored art, and making it rather clear she adored artists. I fell, silly old Cheel, I fell. I made a date with her for last night, and she kept it.'

'Is she a lady?' Cheel asked sombrely.

'There aren't any nowadays, so far as I know. She has a husband who's a City gent, if that means anything. She had to get away from him and from two foul old men in a restaurant, it seems, in order to keep her promise to me. She said she was going to see her old governess.'

For a moment the familiar room in which he was standing swam round Cheel as if it were something ingeniously uncomfortable in a fun-fair.

'Do you know her name?' he asked hoarsely.

'Only her Christian name – if it can be called that. It's Debby.'

'Did you tell her *your* name?'

'Oh, no – just that I was a painter, and had lived in Africa. And I told her to call me Sebastian.'

There was a silence. Through it, Cheel was dimly conscious

of sounds indicative that life elsewhere was pursuing the even tenor of its way. There was a ritual clatter, for instance, as appropriate personnel of the Greater London Council moved down the street, emptying dust-bins. Farther away, a railway-engine was signifying its arrival in the metropolis by an unnecessary but understandable wail of despair. And downstairs, somebody was struggling with one of the obsolete sanitary appliances of the departed substantial citizen.

The room had at least come to anchor. Admit – Cheel told himself – that this new crisis is a stiff one. And then go to work in a cool way to take the measure of it.

English painters with the Christian name of Sebastian and a history of domicile in Africa couldn't be very thick on the ground. Any informed person hearing of such a painter would say 'That must be Sebastian Holme' – and then, presumably, add 'But how odd, since Holme's dead'. This was alarming in itself. But the real mischief, of course, was the fact of Debby's acquaintance with Wuggles. It had the appearance of a fairly close acquaintance. At least Wuggles and Duffy were cronies, and Debby (when not escaping to visit her old governess) was more or less constrained to tag on. Moreover Wuggles himself was already in some way a danger-point. Cheel was convinced of this.

But there was one substantial saving fact. Debby's relationship with Holme was of the most casual order, so far. Moreover it was a disreputably clandestine one. Debby might be excited about her newly acquired artistic bedfellow. But she would hardly be likely to go running off to tell either her husband or her husband's familiar friend about him. At least Cheel supposed not.

Yet, it was true that, with thoroughly depraved people, you never knew. Shocking as it seemed, Cheel had heard of married couples who communicated to each other and to their friends whatever promiscuous encounters came their way. He couldn't be sure that Duffy, Debby and Wuggles didn't belong to a coterie in which such horrors obtained. If this were so, prospects were very bleak indeed. Wutherspoon at least, with his acrid tags

137

from the poets, seemed not altogether a fool. If Debby chattered about her new conquest in his hearing there was no assurance that he wouldn't put two and two together.

But there was one effective hope. The affair might be so ephemeral that nobody would ever think to mention it again to anybody. Cheel felt that he must sound out this possibility with Holme at once.

'Well,' he said, with a forlorn attempt at an indifferent manner, 'I don't suppose you intend to see more of her.'

'That would hardly be possible, old boy.'

'Keep your indecent quips for somebody else!' Cheel's sense of moral decorum was really outraged. 'You don't, I take it, propose another meeting with the woman?'

'Don't I? Let me see. I wouldn't say, mind you, that custom would be incapable of staling her infinite variety. Debby's not exactly a Cleopatra. But, well –' Holme was silent for a moment. He had the air of a man doing sums. 'I'd say there will be six or seven more nights to her, at a guess.'

Although obscurely aware that in this particular speech he was being merely baited, Cheel found it too much for him.

'Abomination!' he cried in a loud voice, and left the room.

Part Three

24

A third day dawned – one destined to be quite as crowded as either of those during which the fortunes of Mervyn Cheel have been exhibited so far. But Cheel himself, knowing nothing of this, lay in bed rather late. The woman who came in to do the cleaning in the morning had now been trained to bring him a little pot of China tea. This was an agreeable start to the day. So was the circumstance that – the lady being plump, good-natured, and not really very far past fifty – a little horse-play could be added to the proceedings from time to time.

But this morning Cheel was in a meditative mood. He was disposed, in fact, to sum up the position to date. Taken all in all, it was satisfactory. Certainly, fortune had taken none of the dire turns that had appeared to threaten from time to time. Sebastian Holme had become, once more, at least moderately well-behaved. He had another working fit on him, and in a day or two there would be a further picture to take to the Da Vinci Gallery. Braunkopf had already disposed of three canvases. 'Clouded Leopards Playing' was the only one at present remaining with him; it was a particularly fine Holme, and he was determined to get a particularly high price for it.

All this was excellent. And none of the people whom it was prudent to keep a wary look-out for had shown any sign of sinister behaviour. If Holme was persisting in his improper relations with Debby the fact was one which Cheel, of course, must deplore. But there had been no ill consequence so far. Debby must be keeping her mouth shut about the glamorous painter, Sebastian from Africa. She'd be a fool if she didn't. Then there was the unspeakable Rumbelow. He, in a sense, was potentially a double threat. On the occasion of his outrageous visit to Cheel's former quarters he had appeared to be on the verge of recalling Holme's identity. And his behaviour at Burlington House – when he had responded with such insane violence to a sophisticated and exquisitely witty joke – had suggested that he might launch himself in implacable vendetta against his adversary. But nothing had happened. Cheel, naturally was keeping his own present whereabouts dark. And perhaps Rumbelow had left town. He possessed – Cheel had discovered – a hovel and a barn-like studio in some God-forsaken corner of Kent. Presumably he manufactured his full-size absurdities there.

This left only Wutherspoon as a focus of real anxiety. The more Cheel looked back on the whole course of events since his first astounded discovery of the living Sebastian Holme, the more (curiously enough) did he sense Wutherspoon's odd explosion at the dinner-table as containing some hidden threat to his whole grand design. Yet this persuasion was almost irrational, and there hadn't been the flicker of an occasion upon which it had in any degree been substantiated.

There was every reason, in fact, for a modest confidence that fortune was behaving as it should, and smiling upon his deserts. Holme, it was true, had been adamant about his £500. But even that sum was already insignificant compared with what had come in. If nothing came unstuck within, say, the next three months Cheel would be in possession of what could only be called a competence. He was already making discreet inquiries from the agents of Swiss banks into the technique of opening a numbered account. He had filled a whole drawer with the proposals of estate-agents anxious to market desirable villas on the Spanish or North African coasts.

It was comfortably enough, then, that Cheel got out of bed eventually and turned on a bath. As he waited for it to fill, his eye fell on an evening paper which he had bought, but scarcely looked at, the night before. There was a minor headline that seemed of interest:

TERRORISTS SCATTERED
WAMBA GOVERNMENT'S SUCCESS

The paragraph following this was very short. JUMBO, it appeared, directed by the atrocious 'Emperor' Mkaka, had again been rearing its ugly head in the paradise of democratic Wamba. But the MADS had the situation well in hand; Professor Ushirombo had held a press conference; it was even believed in informed circles in Wamba-Wamba that Mkaka had been executed by his enraged and disappointed followers; there was likely to be a Royal Visit to Wamba in the spring, when the new Palace of Industry – symbol of the country's now advanced and awakened state – was due to be opened.

Cheel read all this complacently and with a legitimate proprietary interest. He had settled down to a late and substantial breakfast when the telephone-bell rang.

'Here Braunkopf, here Braunkopf – yes?'

Cheel heard this opening with satisfaction. It seemed likely that the owner of the Da Vinci Gallery was about to report that a fat cheque for 'Clouded Leopards Playing' was in the bag.

'Here Cheel,' he replied humorously. 'How are you, my dear fellow?'

'You Cheel come here damn-quick.'

'I beg your pardon?' Cheel was much offended by the words.

'*Und schnell . . . Verstanden? Unverzuglich! Schreckliche Umstände –*'

'Would you mind –'

'*Sofort – verstehen Sie? Dieses eine Wort sage ich dir noch. Beeilen-Sie sich!*'

There was a click and the telephone went dead. Cheel was perturbed. That Braunkopf possessed anything that could be called a native language at all was something that had never entered his head. This tumble of expressive if indifferent German seemed to suggest a sinister degree of psychical trauma. In fact, it sounded very much as if something *had* come unstuck. And

143

Cheel had long ago resolved what he would do when *that* happened. He would collect his current resources, cut his losses, and take the first available flight abroad. And so strong was his instinct that the moment for this had come now that he actually went back to his bedroom to pack a bag. Then he hesitated. Ever since the eleventh century (he recalled) Cheels had been celebrated for the obstinate valour with which they contested the field. Besides, there was still a *very* large sum of money to be made.

And Braunkopf, after all, was an absurd person. It was very conceivable that he was simply putting on a turn over some entirely trivial matter. Even if he had got wind of the truth – to wit, that Sebastian Holme was not dead but alive – he was now so far involved in prevarication about his wares that he was hardly in a position to turn nasty. In selling three Holmes he had three times explained the preservation of a number of the Wamba pictures by repeating Cheel's story to the effect that they had been purchased by a certain ill-fated Mr Kabongo, later liqui-dated by the Wamba State Ballet. Moreover he had never again asked Cheel for the fictitious receipt which Cheel had so rashly averred to be mysteriously in his possession. This had been just as well, since Holme, when tackled, had bluntly refused to fudge up anything of the sort. It was another point adding to what might be called Braunkopf's complicity. There, indeed, lay the beauty of the whole thing. Braunkopf, as much as Holme him-self, was now a helpless accomplice. There could be no real danger in going to see what he was fussing about.

Thus did Cheel, whether through courage or calculation, defy that inner prompting which urged him to immediate flight. He dressed with unusual care and then brought out his magnificent hired car. He still got a great kick out of the Rolls. He felt pretty sure that Braunkopf, despite his unmannerly telephone call, would again be out on the pavement when it was reported as drawing up.

As he slipped into gear he became aware (as once on a previous occasion) of a newspaper poster balanced against a lamp-post. It said:

144

– and then, in smaller type that he didn't quite manage to read, it said something ending either in FLEES or in PEACE. Or was it TREES? Perhaps Ushirombo had established peace, or perhaps JUMBO was in flight – or for that matter had bolted upwards into the branches like the near-monkeys they no doubt were. Cheel chuckled and drove on. He was one not for long daunted, and confidence was returning to him.

And, sure enough, Braunkopf was standing outside the Da Vinci Gallery as he drew up and got out. But so, he then immediately saw, was another man – whom he was unable to persuade himself he liked the look of. There was something unpleasantly stony about the set of his features. Cheel, curiously enough, had never to his knowledge met a plain-clothes detective, and he wondered whether this was what a member of that disagreeable branch of the police looked like. It was perhaps with some idea of flight even at this eleventh hour that he now looked swiftly about him. The result of this survey was only an awareness of two further posters. The first merely read:

'PROFESSOR'
USHIROMBO
SACKED

but the second was more informative:

WAMBA
LIBERATED
DR MKAKA FORMS
GOVERNMENT

'But they can't!' Cheel exclaimed wildly, and as if the matter were of the utmost moment to him. 'They can't have JUMBO, you know. They're mere –'

'Why can't they?' The stony-faced stranger asked this. 'It's a most respectable party. The Joint United Methodist and Baptist Organization, it seems. And the whole country had united against the butcher Ushirombo. Good luck to them.'

'But these are not our concernments, no? We have other fish to fly, yes?' Braunkopf was looking balefully at Cheel as he asked these merely rhetorical questions. Then he waved a commanding hand towards the door of the Da Vinci. 'Vot privileges!' he said with rude irony as Cheel entered. 'Oh, vot happiness!'

25

Cheel had been much too agitated to notice, in the window of the Da Vinci, whatever might there be exhibited as the authentic Braunkopf sculpture of the week. But he was at once aware of the inside of the place as having undergone another of its transformations. The *trecento* and *quattrocento* had vanished. The walls had been hung with a faintly damasked paper of pale lavender. The collection on view appeared to be made up entirely of contemporary English watercolours. And most of these were evidently by a single hand.

Cheel took a look at the hand. It was a hand meticulous in a manner that would appear, superficially, to run counter to the medium. The effects achieved, nevertheless, were very pleasing. This, however, was not what struck Cheel. What struck him was that he could *read* the hand. His professional expertness enabled him to do this at once. And it was the hand – exercising itself, indeed, in a fashion totally new – of Albert Rumbelow.

For a moment Cheel had no other thought than that he had been led into a ghastly trap. He looked desperately around him, in the immediate expectation that Rumbelow was about to leap from behind a settee, brandishing a cane or even a rapier. So strong was this persuasion, that he even turned and began a bolt to the door. But he found that – whether by accident or design – the stony-faced man was in his way. So he thought better of it, and walked on. Flight would now be no good, in any case. They would all be after him in a flash.

Moreover the thing might merely be a coincidence. If Rumbelow had watercolours to exhibit, the Da Vinci was quite a reasonable place in which to display them. Even so, it was unfortunate. Artists have a knack of haunting their own shows. (It was Sebastian Holme's having done so that had drawn Cheel through the first shallows towards those deep waters which – he feared – now threatened to engulf him.) So Rumbelow – even without being apprised of Cheel's visit – might turn up at any minute. It was with relief that Cheel reached the comparative security of Braunkopf's inner sanctum.

But this lasted for no more than seconds. He took a look at the authentic Braunkopf painting of the week, and saw that it was Holme's 'Clouded Leopards Playing'. Then he took a look at the only other painting in the room. It had been set up on a similar easel. And it was Holme's 'Clouded Leopards Playing' too.

There was a long, pregnant silence. And in this it came to Cheel that *he* must speak first. If he could just grasp the initiative, establish a tone, a note – then all might yet be well.

'Fascinating!' he heard himself say. 'A replica, but not *quite* a replica. One can spot at once a slight change in the balance of the composition, and several passages where he hadn't quite satisfied himself first time. And the colour, too, has been modified in places. Look at the yellow flower in the right foreground. Or rather, look at the violet in its shadow. It's not the same violet.'

'That is goot – that is very goot!' Braunkopf nodded his head in altogether sinister concurrence. 'The violet we shall speak about instantly. But first, Cheel, your explainings, yes?'

Cheel was so unnerved (despite his boldness of utterance) that for a moment he almost indulged the preposterous notion of telling the truth. But this unworthy thought he repressed at once.

'I wonder,' he asked, 'if this is something that Holme often did? Since he's dead, and since so much is destroyed, I suppose we shall never know.' He went closer to the pictures. 'I'd say that, if anything, the version that has just turned up on you is the better of the two. Of course, Braunkopf, it sets you a problem from your commercial point of view. One of those puttikler ethical problems that the Da Vinci likes taking in its stride.'

This amiable banter had no apparent mollifying effect upon the Da Vinci's proprietor.

'There is the provenances,' he said. 'This picture has the goot provenance.' He tapped the version of 'Clouded Leopards Playing' that had just so disastrously turned up. 'But this picture' – he tapped the version that Holme had so recently completed – 'has *not* the goot provenance. For it, there is only the cow and hen story of Mr Kabongo who was trampled by heffalumps.'

'Not at all,' Cheel said sharply. He detested inaccuracy. 'Killed by the Wamba State Ballet.' He paused, and then laughed easily. 'But isn't this,' he asked, 'a storm in a tea-cup? Here are two self-evidently authentic Sebastian Holmes – the one being a slightly modified replica of the other. There's nothing out of the way in that. Or do you think one of them is a forgery?'

There was again a silence, but this time it came with a slight effect of bafflement on Braunkopf's part. Braunkopf, indeed, directed a glance of something like appeal at the stony-faced man. But the stony-faced man made no sign whatever.

'And now it's *my* turn to want a little information please.' Cheel put every ounce of assurance he possessed into this bold *tour de force*. 'For I must say quite frankly, Braunkopf, that you have some pretty stiff explaining to do. Be so good as to tell me' – he pointed at the newly appeared Holme – 'just whom you've had this from.'

'From a puttikler eminent dipsomaniac gentleman –'

'Diplomatic,' the stony-faced man said, speaking for the first time since he had entered the Da Vinci.

'Exackly. A diplomatic gentleman direk from Wamba itself. A Mr Wutherspoon.'

For a moment Cheel simply tried to pretend to himself that he hadn't heard correctly. Then he made one of his heroic efforts.

'Ah, yes – I know Wutherspoon. He's a drunk, and an unreliable rascal. Certainly he spent years in Wamba, but he was

148

run out of the country. It would be fatal to believe a word he says.'

'Curiosities, Mr Wutherspoon has never heard of Mr Kabongo. Mr Wutherspoon is agreeable two Holmes saved from the hotel. And they were dissipated –'

'Confiscated,' the stony-faced man said.

'They were confiscated by the government of the Herr Professor Ushirombo and donated this Wutherspoon as compensatings for sudden termination his services. So Wutherspoon having fallen into indigestion –'

'Indigence,' the stony-faced man said.

'– is now obliged ask Da Vinci Gallery market these two surviving Holmes. And here' – Braunkopf again tapped the new painting – 'the first.'

'Well, you must just be careful.' Cheel offered this advice with frank cynicism. 'Nobody's going to pay as much for a painting of which there's an artist's copy as he is if it's known to be unique. And then there's the question of title, you know, of ownership. It seems very probable to me that this fellow Wutherspoon has come by his Holmes through sheer theft.'

'Whereas the honest Mr Kabongo paid two hundert pounts, no?' Braunkopf gave Cheel one of his most disagreeable looks. 'And there is other troublesomes too. There is the suspectings of forgery – as you said, yes?'

'That sort of thing may be said too.' Cheel nodded, and then applied himself at leisure to a further study of first the one and then the other 'Clouded Leopards Playing'. 'Wouldn't you say,' he asked candidly, 'that forgery just has to be ruled out?' He turned from Braunkopf and appealed blandly to the stony-faced man, whom he now rather suspected of being a private eye. 'As an expert, sir,' he said, 'would you not be prepared to stake your reputation that both these paintings are entirely the work of Sebastian Holme?'

'I confess that I should be strongly tempted to do so.' The stony-faced man, it now occurred to Cheel, had a wholly cultivated – indeed what might be called an academic – accent. 'Yet my experience, which is tolerably extensive, tells me, Mr

149

Cheel that there is today no limit to the skill with which the forgery of modern paintings can be carried out. No limit at all.' The stony-faced man in his turn made a further inspection of both 'Clouded Leopards Playing'. 'Or almost no limit at all.'

'But excusings!' Braunkopf had suddenly remembered something. 'The formal introduction, yes? Mr Mervyn Cheel, the eminent critic. Dr Quinn, the eminent chemist.'

Dr Quinn inclined his head gravely. It was rather clear that he didn't terribly like Cheel. And Cheel certainly didn't like him. He was very well aware of one branch of chemistry in connexion with which the name of Quinn was apt to turn up.

'The violet,' Braunkopf went on, with a disagreeable softness. 'The peautiful modest violet, no? Of course it is there in the shadow cast by anythink yellow, yes? And here' – he pointed to what must now be called Wutherspoon's Holme – 'it is *so*.' He turned to the second picture. 'And here, *so*. And your eye is goot, my goot Cheel. *This* violet shadow is not *that* violet shadow. That is the aestheticals. But I too have the goot eye – and the sciences as well. All my life I make the expertises. And I look at this violet in "Clouded Leopards Playing" – in *your* "Clouded Leopards Playing", Cheel –'

'Mine?' There had been something that Cheel didn't at all like in Braunkopf's tone.

'Kabongo's, then.' Braunkopf again tapped the frame of the relevant picture. 'And what do I say? I say "My valued freunt Dr Quinn must have one tiny flake this violet pigment".'

There was another of the horrid silences. And then Dr Quinn himself seemed to feel that things might advantageously be speeded up.

'In a word,' he said, 'I have conducted a micro-analysis of a fragment of paint taken from this picture. And I find that this particular violet comes from a substance first synthesized less than a year ago. It has been available in the colourmen's shops for three months at the most. Sebastian Holme could not possibly have used it during his lifetime. This painting is therefore a forgery. An amazing forgery, but a forgery beyond any shadow of doubt.'

Cheel managed a laugh that sounded uncomfortably shrill to his own ear.

'You've neglected one obvious possibility,' he said. 'And it happens to be the true explanation. When the picture came to me – through confidential channels, I must insist – it proved to be a little damaged. I had to touch it up myself. And I used this paint you are speaking of.'

'Mr Cheel, that is rubbish.' Dr Quinn's face was more granite-like than ever. 'I have also employed radiography, and Mr Braunkopf is now in possession of macrographs of the relevant areas. There has been no damage, and no touching up whatever. Moreover there are the strongest indications that the whole painting has been executed very recently indeed.'

Big men have to be capable of big decisions. Mervyn Cheel was very conscious of this now. What confronted him was, in vulgar parlance, a fair cop. And he had better face up to it at once. Braunkopf, despite his nauseous airs of injured virtue, was already in up to the neck. As for this detestable Quinn, he was clearly a scientist existing on a pittance of a salary, and he was bound, therefore, to have his price.

'Very well,' Cheel said. 'Let us be frank. As you've no doubt guessed, Sebastian Holme is still, in fact –'

But Braunkopf had raised a prohibitory hand – and with such authority that the image of Lord Duveen might have been said positively to shine through him.

'Here,' he said, 'we come to the confidentials. Dr Quinn, my goot freund, it will be correck that you overdraw.'

'Withdraw,' Quinn said unemotionally, and got to his feet. 'I am very content to leave Mr Cheel and yourself to confer.' He paused, gave Cheel a particularly bleak last look (he must be one of those, after all, in whose mind the Nicolaes de Staël affair lingered), and walked out of the room.

Cheel drew a long breath.

'Will he keep his mouth shut?' he asked urgently. 'Can we square him?'

'Mouth shut? Square him?' Braunkopf-Duveen repeated these

151

distasteful expressions while turning upon Cheel the coldest of eyes. 'But you were about to make a communicating, yes?'

'You can call it that, if you like. But you know very well what I have to say. Sebastian Holme is still alive. He's alive, and in London, and painting, now.'

'You make the jokings, Cheel. Always you make the jokings. It is ha-ha-ha, no?' Braunkopf was, in fact, austerely remote from hilarity. 'But this is the tall story, my poor Cheel. It will not take you far.'

'What the devil do you mean?'

'You are a goot forger, Cheel. Perhaps there has never been so goot a forger before. But a goot liar? No.'

26

Very naturally Cheel was as much offended as he was alarmed by this judgement. He was far from flattered by the suggestion that he was a superb forger. In his character as an artist, his high sense of dedication to the practice of abstract *pointillism* made intolerable to him the mere thought of working in any other painter's manner. Conversely, to be denied the highest skill in the craft of prevarication was extremely mortifying to his own just sense of his powers in that direction. What he chiefly felt at the moment, however, was contempt for the gross intellectual incapacity of Braunkopf, whose fixed ideas about the situation were proving invulnerable to the facts of the case. That Sebastian Holme was indeed alive must now be as plain as a pikestaff to any rational intelligence. But here was Braunkopf obstinately pursuing the idiotic notion that Cheel himself could paint, and had been painting, bogus Holmes detectable only through a technical slip.

It was too silly for words. Still, it was evident that the whole grand design must now be reorganized on a drastically different basis. Cheel was about to tell the obtuse proprietor of the Da Vinci Gallery that he was able and willing to produce Holme, active and in the flesh, at half an hour's notice, when he was prevented by a buzzer sounding on Braunkopf's table. Braunkopf picked up a telephone.

'But, yes,' he said. 'But if there was an appointment he must be shown in.' He put down the receiver and turned to Cheel apologetically. 'A client,' he explained. 'A misimportant client. But it would be discourtesies to be longer engaged. You excuse?'

Cheel didn't excuse. He judged it highly improper and inexpedient that a delicate phase in negotiation should be interrupted in this way. But, before he could protest, the door had opened and Braunkopf's visitor entered the room. It was Cheel's former neighbour, the miserable glass-scratcher Binchy.

Once more, coincidence was conceivable. Binchy might be ambitious to follow Rumbelow as an exhibitor in the Da Vinci Gallery. But Cheel doubted it. It wasn't long before he found his dubiety justified.

'Dear me,' Binchy said. 'If it isn't friend Cheel.' He turned to Braunkopf. 'Cheel and I pig together, more or less. He's the attic varlet.'

'But this is interestings.' Braunkopf adopted the air of one indulging in small-talk. 'And you have the artistic communions, yes?'

'Well, we pass the time of day on the stairs. Quite often, I'd say – eh, Cheel? Only the other day, for instance. Yes, only the other day. How is your new activity going, Cheel, old boy?'

'I don't know what you're talking about. I have no new activity. And you know very well that it isn't I who lodges above you any longer.' Cheel's mouth had gone disagreeably dry. He had a sense of what was coming at him. It was conspiracy. 'Everybody in the building must know that.'

'Must they? It's the first I've heard of it. What a funny chap you are! And turning secretive, one might say.'

'Secretive?' Braunkopf repeated softly. 'This too has the interestingness, no?'

'When Cheel hasn't been scribbling rubbish in any rag that would print it, you know, he's been covering perfectly nice little

153

bits of paper and board with spots. Effect rather like the measles. Don't ask me what he does with them afterwards. The Seurat of the sewers, we've always called him. Haven't we, Cheel?'

Cheel was not aware that he had heard this vulgar witticism before. He managed to preserve a dignified silence.

'But lately he's been scurrying round with large canvases. And he says that what he's doing with them is something that nobody will ever *precisely* know. I think those were his words to me quite some time ago. He's a deep one, is Cheel.'

'The goot Cheel has a puttikler prestidigious subtle mind.' Braunkopf produced this with an irony that was highly offensive. 'And we give it damn-plenty employment now.'

'But I must be off myself. My little business with you will keep until you're less occupied, my dear Braunkopf.' Binchy had stood up and was nodding cheerfully. 'Particularly as there's a lady waiting. I'll send her in. And now I'll get back to my lavatory windows and tooth-mugs, Cheel. So long.'

With this parting shot, Binchy walked from the room. There was a moment's murmur of talk outside it, presumably with the waiting lady. And then the waiting lady entered. It was Hedda Holme.

'My goot Mrs Holme, please take place!'

Braunkopf had risen to receive his new visitor, and was bowing in a most Duveen-like way over her hand. His manner, in fact, carried all the respectful deference proper towards one who might still be described with approximate accuracy as a recently bereaved widow.

'I think,' Braunkopf went on, 'you know the man Cheel?'

'Sure. I know Mr Cheel.' Hedda was making her way to a chair while preserving an elaborate care to present only the front part of her person to Braunkopf's other visitor. This semi-public allusion to an entirely private and intimate matter struck Cheel as in very bad taste.

'The man Cheel,' Braunkopf pursued, 'is suffering from a delusion. That, at least, is the charitables. He claims that your sadly departed husband is alive.'

154

'Sebastian's dead,' Hedda said.

'Exackly. Sebastian Holme is dead. Pinched in the bud. Dumped to rest in foreign soil that is forever Englant, no? But Cheel believes otherwise. It seems a case for medical persistence.'

'Isn't it time,' Cheel asked, 'that we dropped this nonsense? If we're all going to get our cut – and I take it that is what this foolery is about – it's high time we had a little straight talk.'

But at this Braunkopf and Hedda only looked at each other sadly.

'Locoed – huh?' Hedda said.

'Either he is mad, Mrs Holme, or he is a knave. And if he is a knave, he has met his Paddington, yes?'

Oddly enough, it was this last fantastic abuse of the Queen's English that finally triggered off righteous anger in the breast of Mervyn Cheel.

'Now, look,' he said. 'If anybody is meeting his Waterloo in this affair, it's you two. I've done nothing – nothing, do you hear? – except place on the market as paintings by Sebastian Holme paintings that are in fact by Sebastian Holme. Whereas what shady tricks you've been up to the police will pretty quickly find out.' He turned to Hedda. 'Didn't you put up a damned lie to the effect that you believed Braunkopf and myself to have all those Wamba pictures stowed away? It was Braunkopf and yourself, all the time. The beastly things were never destroyed, despite your idiotic husband's swearing they were. That ghastly Wutherspoon has one or two of them – but you two have all the rest. And you've been making a fool of me.'

Cheel paused, panting. Braunkopf and Hedda again did no more than exchange commiserating glances. And Cheel pulled himself up. Whatever the true facts of the case, he had to acknowledge that in his last remarks he had been threshing about wildly. It was almost certain that, of the Wamba pictures, only Wutherspoon's couple had really been rescued.

'Listen,' he said. 'I've *got* Sebastian Holme. What's more, I've got him *under my thumb*.' Cheel made a vicious gesture on the

155

table in front of him. 'Sebastian emptied his dead brother Gregory's –'

'His *dead* brother Gregory! Vot ravings, no?' Braunkopf gave an expressive wave of his hands.

'He emptied his dead brother Gregory's bank account on the strength of forged cheques. I can have your blasted Sebastian put inside for a long term tomorrow.'

'Sebastian is dead,' Hedda Holme said.

'Dead,' Braunkopf echoed. 'And dead men is not punishable.' He recollected himself. 'Exceptings,' he added piously, 'by Divine Improvidence.'

'Have some sense!' Cheel's irritation before the obstinate stupidity of these people mounted within him. 'I know very well that you don't *want* him alive. I know that his survival is highly inconvenient to you. It reopens the whole question of what was sold in the Da Vinci here as coming from Mrs Holme's estate as her husband's legatee. But we can fix that. We have a pretty tough hold on him: something like five years in gaol.'

'Sebastian Holme is dead,' Braunkopf said.

'Dead.' This time the echo came from Hedda.

And it pulled Cheel up. He saw – all too belatedly – that he had to take a fresh measure of the situation. Actually, these people knew as well as he did that Sebastian Holme was alive. For what the point was worth, they probably knew too that Gregory Holme was dead.

'The forging of cheques and the forging of paintings,' Braunkopf said, 'is all von, Cheel. And you have forged the paintings of this prestidigious great dead artist Holme. There is the evidences of Dr Quinn. There is the evidences of the goot Binchy. Who goes to gaol?'

'In a sense, we'll keep him dead.' Cheel was urgent again. 'There's no difficulty about that. As soon as he shows signs of wanting to come *publicly* alive, we simply put the screw on him. But there's plenty more painting in him yet. Not Wamba paintings. That's finished. We couldn't market supposed replicas of the whole lot. If you two had only been straight with me' – Cheel

156

ventured on a note of robust reproach – 'we needn't have got into that jam. But why not new paintings? In moderation, you know. It would be unwise to flood the market. Paintings that will simply turn up here and there during the next few years. The provenance may be a bit tricky. But between us we can manage it.'

Again Braunkopf and Hedda glanced at each other. Was it possible, Cheel asked himself, that a flicker of doubt, of cupidity, was already flickering in their eyes? He hoped so.

'So there you are,' he said. 'It will all be plain sailing, believe me.'

'Supposings, my goot Cheel, this misfortunate dead painter were not so.' Braunkopf spoke with the air of one idly interested in beguiling tedium with intellectual speculation. 'Supposings you could take his sorrowing viddow to a blissful reunitings now. And supposings this puttikler authentink genius produced more voonderble contributings the great vorlt of art.' For a moment Braunkopf appeared tempted to linger on this elevated and familiar note. Instead, he descended to a more practical view-point. 'It cannot go on for perpetuities. How you arrange the pay-off, yes?'

It was possibly the brutality, the gangsterdom, lurking in this expression that struck a long suppressed chord in the civilized breast of Mervyn Cheel. For the moment, at least, a new voice spoke in him. And it was the voice of one who hated Sebastian Holme the superb painter, who hated Sebastian Holme the successful lover, very much.

'How?' he repeated with a sudden snarl. 'Batter his skull, or paunch him with a stake. Poison him with ratsbane. Chuck him into a canal. We'll take our choice.'

There was a shocked silence. Cheel himself, although not so weak as to be shocked on his own behalf, did wonder whether his tone had been wholly judicious. After all, they were only small-time crooks – Braunkopf and Hedda Holme. They were incapable of bringing anything like his own boldness and breadth of view to the ultimate facts of the situation. Not that he had himself quite seen the truth until this moment. *The time would come when Sebastian Holme would have to go.*

'Mrs Holme,' Braunkopf murmured, 'vot happiness that your husband was a perisher at the hand of heffalumps, crocodiles, savages, and not left to the mercifuls this eminent critic Cheel!'

The perverse folly of this remark was so evident that Cheel wondered whether to waste time denouncing it. He was still wondering, when an unexpected diversion occurred. The door of Braunkopf's sanctum opened, and the detestable Wutherspoon entered the room.

'Darling!' Wutherspoon cried – and folded Hedda Holme in a tender embrace. 'They told me you were here, my angel. So I hurried to you with feet as fleet as my desire. One of the poets.'

'Wuggie, you honey!' Hedda Holme said.

27

From Wutherspoon, transformed into a lover, it could scarcely be said – with another poet – that the loathsome mask had fallen. His figure hadn't exactly filled out. Indeed, it occurred to Cheel that he ought to be carrying not a neatly rolled umbrella but a scythe and hour-glass. His complexion was as yellow as ever. His features retained the atrabilious cast so congruous with the misogynistic apophthegms which had formerly been current on his lips. But Cheel, thinking back to Burlington House, remembered a detectable disposition on the part of the female called Debby to make eyes at Wutherspoon – and this even (as Cheel now knew) when Debby's thoughts must have been much engaged with somebody else. It must be supposed, then, that Wutherspoon – or Wuggles or (now) Wuggie – was not without power of sexual attraction, revolting as this thought was. And what had happened recently seemed clear enough. Not content with substantially mitigating his penury by the sale of 'Clouded Leopards Playing' and whatever was the other Sebastian Holme he had dishonestly smuggled out of Wamba, Wutherspoon was proposing to cash in on Holme in a big way. He had, in fact, made successful addresses to Holme's supposed widow – on whose behalf Braunkopf had sold a couple of dozen Holmes only a few months ago. Here, in Braunkopf's office, the happy couple were shamelessly engaging in amorous transport now.

'Hedda, darling!' Wutherspoon was saying. 'The party's off. So we can have a lovely lunch together – just you and me.'

'Oh, Wuggie!' Hedda received this news with rapture. 'Isn't that just swell? But why is the party off?'

'It's Debby. She had bad news about her governess. The old lady's chest, it seems. Debby has decided to take her to Jamaica at once. A nice, quiet hotel at Montego Bay.'

'What do you know! Isn't Debby *kind*? But what about Duffy?'

'Duffy? He's arranging to do something for the old headmaster of his private school. That's what he does whenever Debby goes off with her governess. . . . Good God!' Wutherspoon's glance had so far strayed from his charmer as to take in the fact that 'Clouded Leopards Playing' appeared to have reproduced itself by a species of fission. 'What the hell is the meaning of that?'

'It is regrettables, Mr Wutherspoon.' Braunkopf pointed at Cheel. 'You know this infected criminal, yes?'

'I'm damned if I do. But, yes – his name's Mervie. Some sort of hanger-on of old Duffy's. Had dinner with him once. The scoundrel welshed on it.'

'That is expectedness, Mr Wutherspoon. And we have just infected him in forgery. He forges Sebastian Holmes.'

'And says that Sebastian is still alive. Darling, wouldn't that be just awful?' Hedda looked fondly at her beloved. 'It would mean, honey, that we couldn't get married.'

'What outrageous rubbish!' Wutherspoon grasped his umbrella in a manner that reminded Cheel unpleasantly of the ferocious Rumbelow with his cane. His expression was of calculated cunning. 'I myself saw Sebastian Holme killed, as a matter of fact. Of course, your brother-in-law Gregory's alive, isn't he?'

'Sure, honey.'

'Braunkopf – that's right?'

'Puffikt correk, Mr Wutherspoon. Mr Gregory Holme was great assistance Da Vinci Gallery arranging voonderble memorial exhibition his late brother Sebastian.'

'Could Gregory have been impersonating Sebastian, do you think?'

'It is possibles. But I think this Cheel has been making the inventions all on his own.' Braunkopf turned to Cheel. 'You thought you could tear the wool from our eyes, no?'

'Call the police,' Wutherspoon said.

So far, Cheel had failed to utter since the detestable Wutherspoon had entered the room. He was equally outraged and bewildered – and in some danger, indeed, of weakly deciding that the situation was too much for him. But at the mention of the police – grotesque bluff though this could only be – he abruptly found his tongue.

'Isn't it time,' he said, 'that you all dropped this nonsensical charade? We're all in it, you know. Apparently Wutherspoon is in it now. And I don't mind saying at once that I refuse to take that as meaning that I myself get a smaller cut.'

'A smaller cut!' Hedda Holme laughed robustly. 'A larger clip on the ear is what's coming to you, Cheel.'

'But look.' Cheel ignored this vulgar abuse. 'I'll put my card on the table. I'll put my *trump* card on *that* table.' He pointed to the massive medieval object that lent an air of such dignity and substance to Braunkopf's inner retreat, 'I'll fetch Sebastian Holme here now. And with anybody who finds his being alive a trifle inconvenient – well, he and I will consider doing a deal on the spot. Agreed?'

'Sebastian's dead,' Hedda said.

'Dead,' Braunkopf and Wutherspoon said together.

'The man who's alive,' Hedda said, 'is his brother Gregory.'

'His brother Gregory's alive,' Wutherspoon and Braunkopf said.

It is often the strongest intellects that are overcome by spasms of intellectual doubt. Cheel has a spasm of it now. For a fearful moment, that is to say, he found himself almost believing the wicked lie thus unanimously put to him. Was it, after all, so inconceivable? The bearded man he had encountered in the Da Vinci Gallery *ought* to have been Gregory Holme. So *was* he? Had he, for some fiendish and impenetrable reason, pretended to be Sebastian pretending to be himself? Had he carried out this imposture so thoroughly that he had even gashed his hand where he, Cheel, had once gashed Sebastian's? Could Sebastian and Gregory be painters of equal skill, like Jan van Eyck and his mysterious brother Hubert?

With such fantastic speculations did Mervyn Cheel for some moments hither and thither divide the swift mind. But he *knew*, of course, that all this was nonsense. And as soon as he had firmly told himself this, a far more plausible – yet almost equally disastrous – reading of the situation sprang into his mind.

Sebastian Holme had been suborned. The criminal gang that Cheel now realized himself to be up against had somehow got at him. *And they had persuaded him to resume his false identity as Gregory.* This was the explanation of the imbecile chorus – or seemingly imbecile chorus – to which he had been listening. And the object of the criminals was clear. They were going to have him, Cheel, in for forgery. And then they were going to exploit the still living Sebastian for their own ends.

No man likes to be defrauded, cheated, betrayed. Certainly Cheel didn't, since it was very much his persuasion that a kindly Providence had intended that, in these matters, the boot should be on the other foot. But if he was to save himself, and to crush his enemies as they deserved to be crushed, he must act at once. He must grab Holme and make it very clear to him, once more, that the first person to go to gaol for forgery would certainly be the man who had signed his dead brother's cheques. It was inconceivable that Sebastian could successfully sustain the role of Gregory through a criminal trial. Cheel, therefore, could still sink him. And that – it must be made very clear to him – was precisely what Cheel would do if he, Sebastian, didn't quit the enemy's camp at once.

'Now look!' Cheel, steeled for action, had sprung to his feet. 'Sebastian Holme's *alive*. And I've got him – see? And he works to my plan, and to my orders. I agree that you are all in on this now. But it will be on my terms. And now you can sit tight, while I go and fetch him. And don't think he won't be Sebastian. Don't kid yourselves he'll be screaming he's Gregory. He won't. Not when I've shown him where he gets off. And where *you* get off, you rotten lot!'

Cheel turned towards the door. He had reached it when he heard, behind him, what could only be the suppressed laughter of three people. He turned on them in fury.

'I'll be revenged on the whole pack of you!' he screamed. And he rushed from the room.

28

He drove faster than he had ever driven through London before. He had an obscure but strong persuasion that time was now somehow the crux of the whole matter; that this hour was an eleventh hour; that with every minute that went by there was increasing danger that any remaining command of the situation would slip from his grasp. Every now and then he felt a swimming sensation in his head – and when he did so he made a further savage jab at the accelerator. But the car, of course, refused to misbehave. It pretty well ignored him – much as an experienced pony might ignore an excited child behind him in a governess car. Presently it simply came to a halt before his old quarters. Even in his present state of perturbation, he found himself struck by the extremely dismal state into which the place had fallen. To have to live again in the departed citizen's disgraced dwelling was unthinkable. He just wouldn't survive it. But might he not be reduced even to this if his enemies got the better of him? Spurred to frantic energy by this thought, he went upstairs as if a fearful fiend were loping along behind him.

The door of the attic was ajar, and this he knew to be ominous. He pushed inside. As on a former unpropitious occasion, the room was empty. And not only was Sebastian Holme not in evidence. There was no trace of any of his possessions. What of his own property Cheel had left behind him – and it was quite a lot, one way and another – was scattered about as it always had been. But Holme's new clothes weren't in the cupboard, nor were his old ones either. He had vanished without leaving behind him so much as an empty packet of cigarette papers. It was as if he had never been.

It was as if he had never been! Confronting this fact, Cheel realized that his enemies had been at work again. They had spirited Holme away; they had probably as good as locked him up in some fastness of their own; and they had seen to it that there was nothing whatever to which Cheel could point by way of substantiating his claim that Sebastian Holme *existed*.

Once more Cheel's head swam. It was the reversal of his role that was so confusing. He had put all that effort into (so to speak) keeping Holme *dead*. And now it was absolutely necessary to keep him *alive*. He felt that he wouldn't greatly care even if the whole story became public and never yielded another penny again. This would represent, of course, a shocking disappointment to his just hopes. It might even be exceedingly awkward from a legal point of view. But at least it would get him clear of the charge of having painted 'Mourning Dance with Torches', 'Fishing Cats at Pool', 'Clouded Leopards Playing', and several other supposed Sebastian Holmes, himself. He had no illusions about where being convicted of *that* would land him. Moreover he had a strong, irrational, but entirely laudable distaste for the notion of doing, or being taxed with doing, another man's painting. It was true that Sebastian Holme *could paint*; it was true that he could do things with pigment and oil on canvas that Cheel, somehow, just didn't have the knack of. But Cheel *could* do abstract *pointillism*; if he wasn't its inventor he was its refiner

163

and perfecter; and one day his reputation would rise clear of that of all his contemporaries. He would hate to be in any way associated with Sebastian Holme's work. It was superb of its kind, one had to admit. But that sort of thing, after all, was very old hat.

This train of reflection was not, for one in Cheel's present situation, of much utility. Fatigue, perhaps, was telling on him. Certainly he had sat down – and he now fell to staring rather vacantly around him, possessed of a dismal sense that he wasn't even, with any degree of security, back where he started. But from this lethargy he was presently aroused by a step on the stairs. Holme was returning, perhaps, from one of his illicit expeditions. Conceivably he was so returning not as *Sebastian* Holme (which he was) but as *Gregory* Holme (which he wasn't). Cheel stood up. He prepared to do battle.

But the man who entered the attic room wasn't a Holme at all. He was the imbecile cuckold, Duffy.

Duffy seemed to be as surprised to see Cheel as Cheel was to see him. He looked puzzled and disconcerted; it was some seconds before a ghostly simulacrum of jovial recognition flickered in his features.

'Hullo, hullo!' he said. 'Fancy running into you. Haven't seen each other, have we, since jolly old St Tropez?'

'Yes,' Cheel said. 'We have.' This wasn't, conceivably, a wise retort. It was sheer irritation and an impulse to tart contradiction that produced it. And malice made Cheel add: 'How's Debby?'

'Debby? Much as usual, I'd say. Taken an old lady away on a holiday, as a matter of fact. Only I rather thought she might be here.'

'Here? What should make you think that?'

'Well, I've stumbled on the address. It seems Debby's been coming along here – I suppose to see this old woman. I thought I might catch her.'

'Catch her?'

'Oh, just with a message before she went off.' Duffy was staring

164

about him. He seemed confused or ill at ease. 'You know,' he said, 'things are deucedly tiresome. Is this where *you* live?'

'Yes,' Cheel said. 'I mean, no. I did once.'

'Odd. I don't see that Debby could possibly take an interest –' Duffy checked himself. 'Something about you,' he said, 'that I'd like to remember. Any idea what it can be?'

'No. None whatever. And, as you've made some mistake, you'd better go away.'

'Go away? Well, I am – as a matter of fact.' Duffy brightened. 'Taking somebody on a holiday. Spot of charity, really. The decent thing, now and then.'

'No doubt,' Cheel said. His impatience with Duffy (and Duffy's old schoolmaster) was extreme. 'Try St Tropez.'

'My God – it's come back to me!' Duffy had suddenly pointed an accusing index-finger at Cheel. 'That dinner, you know. With Debby and old Wuggles. Your treat. And you cut out of it.'

'I don't know what you're talking about.'

'There you are – trying to cut out again. Not the thing, old boy. Not the thing at all. Not as if you were on your uppers. I remember the style you kept up at jolly old –'

'You don't remember anything of the sort. I've never been there. I wouldn't be seen dead in the vulgar place. Now, go away.'

'It won't do, Mervie. I remember your name now. And I remember your car, too. In fact, I've just noticed it outside this house. Be a man, Mr Mervie, and cough up.'

'I'm not Mr Mervie. I'm –'

'I don't care who you are.' Duffy – perhaps because domestic matters were preying on his mind – showed signs of departing from his customary good cheer. 'Sixteen quid and a bit. Allowing for the tips, we'll call it a round eighteen. And I'll collect now. In cash, Mr Mervie. Fellows with cars like yours carry plenty of that around.'

As far as Cheel was concerned, this was, as it happened, a sociological observation of some exactness. A resourceful man is prepared for any emergency. Cheel carried on his person, in ten-pound notes, a very considerable sum indeed. And Duffy was

165

now looking so threatening that Cheel judged himself to be in some danger of suffering physical violence. Without further words, therefore, he took out his pocket-book and paid up. Had he attempted speech, indeed, he would probably have found his voice strangled with rage.

'Thanks a lot, old man.' Duffy's equanimity was instantly restored – a circumstance that was very far from restoring Cheel's. 'See you down there next year, perhaps?'

'I'll see you in hell,' Cheel managed to say.

'Never heard of it.' Duffy looked puzzled. 'Or is it that little place near Hyéres? Well, so long.' He opened the door and went out. Then, momentarily, he stuck his head in again. 'Another visitor coming upstairs,' he said. 'Wonder if you owe him a spot, too? Bye-bye.'

There was certainly the sound of ascending footsteps. And they had passed the floor below. Cheel found himself backing towards a corner of the room. His prescient soul foretold more trouble.

And his prescient soul was right. The door opened again. Framed in it was the dreaded form of Rumbelow.

'Hither to me,' Rumbelow said.

29

Mephistopheles had spoken. Cheel was too alarmed to consider it a poor joke, or even to resent the disagreeable humour with which Rumbelow accompanied his summons with a devilishly beckoning finger. But his position, he obscurely knew, was not precisely that of Faust at the end of the old play. In his case, there was some infernal bargain yet in the making.

'What do you mean?' Cheel said weakly. 'I'm waiting for someone.'

'Yes, but for someone who won't turn up.' Rumbelow brought an ancient gold watch from a pocket, and consulted it. 'One may calculate,' he said, 'that Sebastian Holme is now somewhere

166

over the Mediterranean. So, I am sorry to say, is the wife of that corpulent person I have just passed on the stairs. It would be well for you if you, too, were at least as far away as that. But you are not.'

'It's Holme who had gone off with Debby? I thought so! But I'll get him back.' Cheel produced this with what, in melodramatic fiction, would be termed a snarl. 'He's a forger. He's stolen his brother's money. He's –'

'The real forgery in the case, Cheel, has been going on in this room. When you haven't been wandering about, insulting honest artists in public places, you've been forging paintings by Sebastian Holme. A very large-scale affair. I have taken well-qualified advice, and I am told it might get you five to seven years.'

'It's a lie, and you know it is! Holme has had this room as his studio, and has painted a number of things to replace others that were destroyed. His own survival had to be a secret, because they were after him in Wamba. I've done nothing but help the poor fellow along, and now he repays me by this foul trick.' Cheel's voice broke. He was overwhelmed by an enormous sense of injury. 'And that scoundrel, Braunkopf –'

'I have just come, as it happens, from the Da Vinci Gallery. As you know, some of my current minor work is being exhibited there. I looked in this morning, and was drawn into what may be termed a conference of persons having some concern with your affairs. I gained much information. I gained one crucial piece of information. Your malignity, it appears, has not stopped short of proposing murder, or something like it. This final circumstance has brought me to my present resolution. It is the reason of our leaving here together – as we shall now do.'

'You're crazy! I refuse to have anything to do with you. And I can prove that Sebastian Holme has been here.'

'I think not. By the way, his present destination, as you have no doubt gathered, is Wamba. Wamba-Wamba, as a matter of fact.'

'Rubbish! You're trying to trick me. I tell you, they're after him in Wamba. That was the start of the whole thing. He seduced some top man's wife.'

167

'Quite so. The so-called "Professor" Ushirombo's wife. But Ushirombo's government, as you must have heard, has been overthrown. Power has passed to Dr Mkaka. As it happens, I have considerable influence with him. His artistic taste seems to be such that he highly approves of the designs I have been preparing for the Wamba Palace of Industry. I am in radio communication with him now.'

'I don't believe a word of it! An obscure old dauber like you couldn't have influence with anybody.'

'We shall see. I am quite sure that the Prime Minister – Dr Mkaka himself, that is – will find that Sebastian Holme was not killed. He will also find that he never left Wamba. In fact, the admirably liberal and humane Mkaka will have rescued Holme from a dungeon in which he has been languishing ever since power was seized by the ruthless tyrant Ushirombo. Dr Mkaka will rehabilitate him, and Sebastian Holme will be able to take up his career where he left off. Any story that he has been in England will – as you can see – simply be laughed out of court.'

'You devil!' Cheel cast about in his mind for some last ditch in which to stand. 'There's Gregory Holme. He's supposed to be alive. If it wasn't the live Sebastian cashing Gregory's cheques in England, then it was Gregory himself. But you won't be able to produce him.'

'Producing Gregory Holme is no responsibility of mine. And remember that he was a celebrated explorer. Such people can vanish for years without exciting much remark. Sometimes, they never turn up again. And now, Cheel, are you ready? You won't need any possessions.'

'What the hell do you mean? Are you off your rocker, and thinking of a little quiet murder on your own account? Of course I'm not going with you anywhere.'

'In that case I must call the police. I noticed a telephone in the hall downstairs. So don't think you can get away. Or not for those five years or so. It will be a remarkable case.'

'You can do what you please. I've got money. I'll fight.'

'The sensation will be all the greater. You'll even acquire fame

168

of a sort, Cheel. Like that Dutch rascal, van Meegeren – whose own painting was hopelessly third-rate, but who forged Vermeers superbly.'

'No – not that!' Cheel's voice rose in a scream. 'Anything but that!'

'Then come quietly. It is convenient that you have that powerful car at the door. We have some way to go.'

'Blackheath and Shooters Hill,' Rumbelow said, when they were in the Rolls. 'The road having been made by the Romans – it is in fact Watling Street – remains very tolerable. We then continue down the A2 to Cobham. Were our expedition one of pleasure, we might visit the parish church there and inspect the brasses. They are perhaps the finest in the country. I am remarking the controls as you drive, by the way. You understand that I shall be returning alone.'

Cheel was in no mood for antiquarian conversation. As for Rumbelow's returning alone, he was wondering, on the contrary, whether he couldn't turn down a deserted country lane, batter the old fiend's head in, and bury him. But such crude crimes, he remembered, seldom pass undetected. Moreover there were those other people: Braunkopf, Hedda, the nasty Wuggles. He couldn't liquidate the lot.

These considerations obliged him to abandon any thought of violence as impracticable. This was a pity, since their eventual destination – which was, of course, Rumbelow's retreat in the heart of Kent – held a dismal seclusion just right for crime. They got out of the car between a small wooden cottage and a large wooden barn. There was nothing else in sight.

'The cottage,' Rumbelow said, 'is in some disrepair. The roof leaks – but not to any point of positive inconvenience. Ample water may be pumped from the well at the bottom of the garden.' He led the way inside. 'For cookery of the simpler sort, as you will see, the facilities are not unreasonable. It is possible that I may provide a second saucepan.'

'What the devil do you think this has to do with me?'

'These, Cheel, are your living quarters for the next two years. My age asks ease; and for the completion of my colossal canvases for the Wamba Palace of Industry I am constrained, unfortunately, to employ an assistant. This the Wamba authorities understand. I have explained to them that it was the practice of many Old Masters. You, Cheel, are to be my assistant. You will work strictly to my instructions – and, of course, on the more routine and detailed parts of the work. We will now go into the studio.'

Numbly, and as a slave behind his master, Cheel followed Rumbelow into the barn. It had been provided with a large north light and a small oil stove, but appeared otherwise untouched. Down two of its sides were enormous canvases on elaborately braced stretchers. Rumbelow paused before the first of these.

'Her Majesty the Queen,' he said, 'reading the Speech from the Throne on the occasion of the State Opening of Parliament. As you will see, most of the Lords are already completed. But some hundreds of Commons, standing at the Bar of the House, have yet to be filled in. Their photographs are available. Now look at the next. It is the new road bridge over the Firth of Forth, viewed from the east and through the cantilevers of the old railway bridge. I flatter myself that the design is intricate and pleasing. But, of course, the number of rivets requiring represen-tation is almost burdensomely large. No doubt you will pass alternately between the rivets and the faces of the M.P.s. They are about equally expressive, after all.'

Cheel was now weeping quietly.

'But I can't,' he wailed. 'I just *can't*!'

'Not at all. Your abilities are very respectable. If honestly applied, they shall receive suitable recompense. I shall, I need hardly say, impound your cash and your cheque-book. It would be foolish to encourage you in the futile notion that flight is a possibility open to you. Your provisions will be delivered by an old woman from the village. She is deaf as well as blind, I am sorry to say. But she finds her way about remarkably well. There will be unlimited bread, cheese and milk. Should your progress herit it, there may later be a small weekly supply of bottled beer. Nothing more, I think, need be said at present. Except to impress upon you, Cheel, that I act out of a reformatory as well as a punitive intention. In two years' time I hope you will be a better man. At least you can hardly be a worse.'

There was a long silence. Then Mervyn Cheel braced himself for one more struggle to make terms.

'Please' – he said piteously – 'you won't *tell*? That's all I stipulate for.'

'You are not in a position to stipulate for anything.'

'It's all I beg. That nobody should *know*.' He pointed, blindly and not very tactfully, at the two vast canvases. 'That nobody should ever know that I have set a hand to these things.'

'Very well. There is no reason why my assistant – although his existence must be admitted – should not retain his personal anonymity. Therefore I agree – subject to your good conduct, of course.'

'Of course, of course.' Cheel was finding that rage and malignity appeared to have been battered out of him. His punishment – what this dreadful tyrant thought of as his punishment – was going to consist of discomfort, boredom and humiliation. Yet, staunch to himself, he was rational to the last. It was all very horrid. But it was better than being put in gaol.

Five minutes later, he watched Rumbelow climb into the Rolls and drive away. Then he turned back to what Hildebert Braunkopf would have called the voonderble vorlt of art.

More About Penguins and Pelicans

Penguinews, which appears every month, contains details of all the new books issued by Penguins as they are published. From time to time it is supplemented by *Penguins in Print*, which is our complete list of almost 5,000 titles.

A specimen copy of *Penguinews* will be sent to you free on request. Please write to Dept EP, Penguin Books, Ltd, Harmondsworth, Middlesex, for your copy.

In the U.S.A.: For a complete list of books available from Penguin in the United States write to Dept CS, Penguin Books Inc., 7110 Ambassador Road, Baltimore, Maryland 21207.

In Canada: For a complete list of books available from Penguin in Canada write to Penguin Books Canada Ltd, 41 Steelcase Road West, Markham, Ontario.

Nicholas Freeling in Penguins

Criminal Conversation
Gun Before Butter
The Dresden Green
A Long Silence
Over the High Side
Strike Out Where Not Applicable
Tsing-Boum

The above titles are not for sale in the U.S.A.
The titles listed below are for sale in the U.S.A.

Because of the Cats
Double-Barrel
King of the Rainy Country
Love in Amsterdam

Michael Innes

'Mr Innes can write any other detective novelist out of
sight. His books will stand reading again and again' –
Time and Tide

'The most able writer of grotesque fantasy in crime fiction'
– *Birmingham Post*

'A master – he constructs a plot that twists and turns like
an electric eel: it gives you shock upon shock and you
cannot let go' – *The Times Literary Supplement*

'The intellectual, the phantasmagoric, the exhilarating
Mr Innes' – *Church Times*

*The following books by Michael Innes have been published
in both Britain and the U.S.A.:*

An Awkward Lie
From London Far
What Happened at Hazelwood